CHRISTMAS STORM

Amish Romance

HANNAH MILLER

Copyright © 2024 by Tica House Publishing LLC

All rights reserved.

No part of this book may be reproduced in any form or by any electronic or mechanical means, including information storage and retrieval systems, without written permission from the author, except for the use of brief quotations in a book review.

Personal Word from the Author

To My Dear Readers,

How exciting that you have chosen one of my books to read. Thank you! I am proud to now be part of the team of writers at Tica House Publishing who work joyfully to bring you stories of hope, faith, courage, and love.

Please feel free to contact me as I love to hear from my readers. I would like to personally invite you to sign up for updates and to become part of our **Exclusive Reader Club** —it's completely Free to join! Hope to see you there!

With love,

Hannah Miller

VISIT HERE to Join our Reader's Club and to Receive Tica House Updates:

https://amish.subscribemenow.com/

Contents

Personal Word from the Author	1
Chapter 1	4
Chapter 2	11
Chapter 3	19
Chapter 4	26
Chapter 5	32
Chapter 6	39
Chapter 7	48
Chapter 8	58
Chapter 9	65
Chapter 10	71
Chapter 11	79
Chapter 12	88
Chapter 13	95
Chapter 14	102
Epilogue	114
Continue Reading...	121
Thank you for Reading	124
More Amish Romance from Hannah Miller	125
About the Author	127

Chapter One

Susan Miller sighed as her father turned the horse into Widow Naomi's driveway. Her nose and fingers were cold from the bite of the early morning temperatures. For the first week of November, it was unusually cold. At least, the widow's house would be warm and cozy.

"I wish you and *Mamm* didn't have to go to Pennsylvania."

"I wish that too, *dochder*. But a person must go when *familye* needs them." Her father smiled at her to reassure her. "Besides, you'll be a big help to Widow Naomi. She's up there in years now and has a much harder time. With winter coming on, you'll be a blessing to her."

His big bay buggy horse trotted up to the house, and her father stopped the buggy. "Let's get your bags," he said.

Naomi came outside to greet them. She had a thick purple shawl wrapped around her thin shoulders and a wide smile of greeting. She walked carefully over the frozen ground. Naomi was frail but had a tough spirit and an eagerness to help anyone who needed it. She was shorter than Susan by a couple of inches and so thin she looked like a strong wind could blow her into the next town. Her once brown hair was mostly gray, and wrinkles creased her face. But her tawny-colored eyes were warm and welcoming.

"Susan, I'm so glad to see you." She caught Susan's cold hands in her warm ones and squeezed gently. "You have *nee* idea how I've been looking forward to today."

"I'm glad," Susan said. "I know we'll enjoy each other's company this winter."

Her father smiled approval.

At least, she was staying with someone who would be glad to have her company. And everyone knew Widow Naomi was sweeter than pie.

Her father took her bags out of the buggy, two of them in one of his big hands and one in the other. He carried them to the door, and the widow held it open for him. He set Susan's bags inside.

"Well, my dear, I must go pick up your mother and your cousin so he can drive the buggy back to the farm after he takes us to the bus station. He folded her in a tight hug.

"We'll see you in the spring. *Denke*, Widow Naomi. We appreciate this so much. I know our Susan will be in *gut* hands."

Naomi nodded. "It's my pleasure to have her here with me."

"Have a safe journey," Susan said and fought not to cry.

He smiled and then hurried to the buggy and headed down the drive.

"Let's go inside where it's warm," Naomi said and led the way into her charming blue and white kitchen. "Would you like a cup of *kaffe* or tea?"

"Either would be *wunderbaar*," Susan said. "I can make it for us if you show me where you keep it."

"I'll make it, dear. But you can see which cabinet I keep it in. That way you can make some whenever you like." She shuffled to the cabinet closest to the gas-powered refrigerator and took out the coffee can. "The tea is right beside it."

Naomi prepared the coffee and set it on the stove. "While the water is heating, I'll show you to your room, and you can bring your bags and put them in there.

Susan settled in quickly. Naomi was pleasant and easy to get along with, and they had a nice routine almost immediately. Naomi had an older cart pony, a flock of chickens, a few cats and an elderly dog. Now that it was cold and sometimes slippery underfoot, Susan had taken over caring for the animals.

And she didn't stop there. She chopped kindling, carried in wood, cleaned out the chicken coop, and got the old pony's stall ready for her each day.

She had gone out one morning to care for the animals when she spied a young woman next door struggling to lead a big draft horse that didn't want to move. She was wiping her eyes and appeared to be weeping.

Susan hurried over to her. "Do you need help? Are you okay?"

The young woman looked at her with such gratitude that it touched Susan's heart.

"Let me help you. Where do you want this horse?"

"In the pasture over there." The woman pointed to the open gate. "But I don't think you'll get him to move. He's too big."

"There's a trick to getting a balky horse to move," Susan said.

She took the lead rope and instead of pulling the horse forward, she pulled him to the side and off balance. He took a step, and she quickly started him toward the gate. After a dozen or so steps, he tried balking again. Susan pulled him off balance again and got him moving. And that time she got him into the pasture and closed the gate behind him.

"*Denke. Ach*, my goodness. I never would have gotten him in there. I don't know what I would have done."

"I'm Susan Miller. I'm spending the winter with Widow Naomi. If you need help with him again, just come get me."

"I'm Nancy Zook. My husband's away working in another town to make some extra money. Do you want to come in? My *boppli* will wake up any time now, and I need to be there for him. I must get all my morning chores done while he's asleep."

"I'd love to come in for a minute."

"I can make *kaffe*," Nancy said.

"That would be nice. I can't stay long though. I don't want Widow Naomi to worry about me."

"We should have time for a cup of *kaffe*. Or you could run and tell her you're going to visit for a few minutes," Nancy said.

"I'm going to tell her. I'll just be a moment."

She hurried back and found Naomi in the kitchen with her chair close to the wood stove. She already had a large pot of vegetable soup cooking.

"I met the girl next door. I'm going over to have a cup of *kaffe*. Then I'll be right back."

"Take your time," Naomi said. "Nancy's a sweet girl. Besides, we don't have anything pressing to do today."

"I know. But I won't be too long." She hurried back outside and over to Nancy who was waiting for her on the front porch.

"Let's go have some *kaffe* and chat," Nancy said and ushered Susan inside her small house. Everything looked spotless and in order.

Susan followed her to the kitchen which was clean but sparse.

"Make yourself comfortable, and I'll get the water heating. Ivan will wake up soon, and I'll have to tend him. I didn't know how difficult things were going to be when my husband went to work away from home."

Susan thought she was going to cry, but Nancy blinked hard and went to fetch sugar and milk for their coffee.

"Is there anything I can do to help?" Susan said.

"I don't think so. But I really appreciate the offer," Nancy said

It had to be difficult. She'd been left with everything a husband would normally do, plus her own work, and a baby to take care of on top of that.

"How old is your son?" Susan asked. Motherhood sounded wonderful to her. It was the highest level a woman could aspire to. At least, as far as those in her district were concerned.

"Ivan just turned a month old," Nancy said.

"*Ach*, he's practically a newborn," Susan said. "You shouldn't have to do everything outside and take care of a tiny *boppli*. How many animals do you have?"

"The usual," Nancy said. "We have a flock of chickens, three horses, a mule, four goats, and a couple cows."

They had too many animals for a new mother to have to deal with every day. Nancy's husband should be doing that.

"I take care of the Widow Naomi's animals every day. I could come over and take care of yours. That would help you out." It just made sense. There was no good reason she shouldn't do it for Nancy. The poor girl looked exhausted and no doubt, she was. Not only that, she hadn't been able to move the horse which meant she likely wasn't really knowledgeable about it. Clearly, she needed help.

"I couldn't ask you to do that," Nancy said.

"You didn't ask. I volunteered. You should be in the *haus* with Ivan, taking care of him and working inside. I take care of the animals at Naomi's. I can just walk over and feed the animals here and take care of anything else they need. It isn't a hardship. And I don't mind doing it."

Nancy said, "If you truly don't mind, you would be a gift straight from *Gott*."

"Then consider it a done deal," Susan said. She smiled at Nancy. The poor girl was overwhelmed. If Susan could help, she would.

Chapter Two

Early that morning, Ezra Fisher packed a couple bags and harnessed his horse. He hummed a hymn as he got his horse ready for the drive to his grandmother's home. He hadn't seen her in a while, and it had been weighing heavily on his heart.

She was an elder and alone. If he lived closer, he could see her more often, but it was an hour drive, each way. And he had so much work as a buggy maker that he'd been putting off leaving his work, fearing he would get too far behind.

But in doing so, he felt he'd neglected his grandmother. What better way to make up for it than by spending the holidays with her and fixing up her place while he was there.

He only had one horse, so at least he didn't have to find someone to take care of his animals for him. Other than getting the necessary time, traveling would be easy for him.

He tossed his bags in the back of the buggy and climbed onto the seat. "Come on, Chief," he said to the big sorrel horse. "Let's go see *Grossmammi*."

Exactly one hour and twelve minutes after Ezra left home, he pulled into his grandmother's driveway. A stream of wood-smoke rose from the chimney, and a plump cat scampered across the driveway. Otherwise, the little farm was quiet.

He stopped the horse and jumped down. Whistling, he sauntered to the door and knocked.

A moment later, the door opened and a lovely young woman with rich chestnut hair and the deepest shade of hazel-colored eyes he'd ever seen peered out at him.

"*Ach*," he said, startled. "Hello, I'm Ezra Fisher. I was expecting my *grossmammi*."

"I'm Susan Miller. I'm staying with Naomi while my parents are away helping relatives." She smiled. "Please, come in. She's in the parlor."

He stepped inside. He was slightly rattled. He hadn't written to his grandmother before coming to visit. He'd just assumed everything was as it always had been so there was no need to contact her first. But now he was an unexpected guest when she already had a guest.

"Well, it's nice to meet you," he said.

"Nice to meet you, too," she said. "Come to the parlor. I'm sure she'll be thrilled to see you."

He followed her into the parlor. His grandmother sat close to the woodstove with her knitting needles and a skein of yarn.

She glanced up and a huge smile broke over her face. "Ezra, my dear boy. Whatever are you doing here?" She stood and embraced him. Her hold on him didn't seem as strong as the last time she'd hugged him—that had been several months back. He was glad he'd come to see her.

She gestured to the sofa. "Sit and tell me the news."

He shucked off his coat and sat on the old but comfortable sofa.

Susan sat beside the large window that overlooked her now empty flower garden.

"I've come to visit through the holidays. I should have written. I had *nee* idea you had a guest." He felt foolish for assuming his grandmother was sitting there all alone pining for someone to talk to.

"That isn't a problem," she said. "This old *haus* has plenty of room. We'd love the company."

He glanced over at Susan. Unlike his grandmother, she wasn't smiling. He wasn't so sure how she felt about it. Well, there wasn't anything he could do, short of going back home, and he wasn't going to do that. He'd come with the intention of helping his grandmother, and he was going to do so.

He really didn't care if Susan wasn't thrilled with him being there, because he wasn't exactly happy she was there either.

"How's your business coming along?" his grandmother asked.

"I'm doing well. I have so much work that this is the first time in a long time I've had enough time to take a trip." He should have made time to come see her sooner. His customers would have waited on orders, for his buggies were in demand for the quality he put in them.

She nodded. "That's *wunderbaar* that you're doing so well. Last time I saw you, you had back orders."

"I remember. *Dat* still helps me when I get into a jam with orders."

She smiled. "Your father always had all the business he could handle."

"Speaking of buggies, I should unhitch my horse."

"The stalls are clean," Susan said. "Put your horse in the barn, and you can give him some hay."

His grandmother nodded.

"I'll be back as soon as I get my horse settled in," he said and pulled his coat on.

"Do you need any help?" Susan said.

He snorted. "Heavens *nee*."

She looked offended.

Well, he hadn't meant anything by it, but goodness, he knew his way around the farm. And he surely didn't need help unharnessing his horse. So she didn't need to sit there and look like she was about to poke her lip out at him. If anyone should be annoyed, it was him. She was a stranger, not family.

He went out and led Chief close to the barn and unhitched him from the buggy. Then he walked him to the barn. He slid the big door open and took Chief inside where it was much warmer.

A bay pony stood in one stall munching hay.

Ezra led Chief to the stall next to the pony and stripped off the harness. He found a curry brush and groomed Chief before getting hay for him. He filled a bucket with water and hung it in the stall.

He checked the stall latch then went back to the buggy to collect his bags.

The following morning, Ezra went to care for Chief and found Susan there feeding the chickens.

"I gave your horse hay and water," she said. "There's grain in the barn, but I didn't know if you give him sweet feed."

"I do give him grain. I'll buy some to replace what he eats. I think I'll turn him out later."

"You can't, the fence is down in the back. I would have fixed it, but I couldn't lift any of the extra fence posts."

"It needs a new post?" he said.

"*Jah*. She has several. But they're big and too heavy for me to manage."

"I can set a post," he said. "This needs to be fixed." And wasn't that why he was there, to help his grandmother?

"I can help with the wire," Susan said.

At least she was willing to help, which he grudgingly admitted would be nice. "All right. That'd be appreciated," he said. "Are you about finished feeding the animals?"

"I am," she said. "I just need to give the goats their feed."

He nodded. "Finish up while I look for some tools to stretch the fence."

"All the tools and the posts are in the shed behind the barn," she said.

Well, she certainly knew her way around the farm. Perhaps that was a good thing. If she was going to stay there for months, at least she was trying to be helpful. On the other hand, he wanted to be the one to help his grandmother. "I'll get the tools and a post."

He went to the shed and found the fence plyers, a spool of wire, and everything else they needed to set a new post and repair the break in the fence. The posts were leaning against the wall in a corner.

He needed a wheelbarrow to take the rest of the supplies in one trip. He went back to the main barn and got the wheelbarrow and filled it with everything they would need to make a repair.

"I'm finished feeding the animals," she said.

"*Gut*. Let's go," he said.

"Okay, we'll fix the fence. And then if you want to help me further, I'd like to replace that loose step on the porch."

"*Jah,* I can help with that too. I was worried about it giving way and someone falling," she said.

"I don't need *Grossmammi* getting injured. I want to help in any way I can while I'm here." He didn't truly need Susan's help, but there was nothing he could do about it. And it seemed she was well settled in. It was a good arrangement for her and his grandmother. And he shouldn't have negative feelings toward her. She was a nice girl.

Still, he wanted to do things himself. But it was what it was, and he couldn't do anything except make the best of the situation.

By the time they finished the fence, he had to give Susan credit. She'd worked hard to help him do a good job. She'd stretched the wire like a pro while he stapled it to the new post. She learned fast, and did everything she needed to help him get it done correctly.

They put away the fencing tools and headed for the porch so they could repair the weak step. He pulled away the old step and sawed a new one to the proper size and fitted it to the stair stringer and riser.

She held the step while he nailed it into place. When they finished, he stood back and looked at their work.

"We've done a lot of work today," he said. "And it's not even noon yet."

"And we did a *gut* job," she said, grinning.

"My girlfriend, Rebecca, couldn't have done all that," he said. "You'd make a *gut* farm helper for someone."

He smiled at her, but it faltered when he saw her furrowed brow and frown.

Chapter Three

Two days later, Susan shivered inside her coat and gloves as she cared for Naomi's animals. Ominous gray clouds filled the sky, and a biting cold wind ripped at the tall grass in the fields, bending it over until it was nearly flattened on the frozen ground.

Once she'd finished taking care of the animals on the farm, she hurried next door to feed and water Nancy's animals.

She was lugging a full bucket of water she'd drawn from the well when Ezra ran across to Nancy's house.

"What are you doing?" he asked.

"I'm feeding Nancy's animals. I take care of them for her. She has a *boppli*, and her husband is working in another community."

"Give me that bucket. I'll help you," he said.

Surprised by his offer, she let him take it from her.

"Where were you headed with this?" he said.

"It's for her chickens. Their coop is next to the barn."

"It's freezing out here," he said. "Let's get this done and get back in the *haus* so we can thaw out. You must be cold. I saw you feeding *Grossmammi's* animals earlier."

"I am pretty cold," she said. Her hands and feet felt half frozen. "*Denke* for helping me. I appreciate it. You couldn't have come at a better time."

She snuck a sideways glance at him. He was certainly handsome—with golden-blonde hair, deep blue eyes, and features filled with youth and vigor. He was about a foot taller than she, and he looked strong; he clearly wasn't a stranger to hard work.

"You should have said something. I would have come with you so you could get done quicker. It's going to snow any minute now."

"How do you know?" she asked.

"Well, there are signs, if you pay attention to them," he said. "Listen, it's so quiet. It's always quiet when it's going to snow. The birds and animals already know, and they're seeking shelter."

"I have noticed that sometimes after a snow it's really quiet," she said.

He nodded. "It's like the snow muffles everything."

"*Jah*, that's it," she said.

"Also," he said. "When it's going to snow a lot, the air feels heavy with it. It's like that right now."

"You're right," she said. She couldn't help but be impressed with his observations.

"My grandfather knew a lot about weather, and he taught me some things about it. Did you ever notice that when it's going to rain the leaves on trees will curl up a little bit?"

"*Nee*. I haven't noticed that."

"It's true," he responded. "When late spring comes, you can check this easily. When you think it's going to rain, look at the leaves on the trees. You'll know for sure if they look curled up."

They reached the barn where the horses were stabled.

"I already took care of the horses," she said. "But the chicken feed and goat feed are stored in there." She hurried in and got a half bucket of chicken feed and hurried to the coop.

He'd already poured fresh water for the chickens.

She filled the feeders then checked for eggs, collecting three.

"We still have the goats and cows to feed," she said.

She put the eggs in a small basket.

"Can you feed the cows? Just take a half-bale of hay to them and two buckets of cow feed. It's in the wooden bin next to the hay bales," she said. "I'll feed the goats."

"Sure, I'll do that," he said.

Between them, they finished quickly.

"I need to take the eggs in and say *hello*," she said.

"I'll wait for you," he said.

"I'll be as quick as I can." She hurried toward the small house.

By the time Susan and Ezra went back to Naomi's, the first tiny flakes of snow started floating down. Ezra went to the kitchen to make hot chocolate. Susan went to the parlor to spend time with Naomi.

She was glad the feeding was done until evening. It had been freezing cold when they went out. But it was even colder by the time they'd finished.

Naomi sat by the wood stove in the parlor and crocheted. She was making a pretty throw for the couch in tan, orange, and gold. The colors of fall, her favorite time of year.

"It's so nice and warm in here," Naomi said. "I'm glad you two brought so much wood in over the last few days. I have a feeling this snow's going to be bad."

"It could be," Ezra said. "It's right cold and windy out."

"Those tiny flakes seem to come when it's going to snow for a long time," Naomi said. "I remember when I was around Susan's age. Poor old Mr. Brown went to help a cow that had gone down and couldn't get up. It was bitterly cold, and those little flakes were coming fast. That poor old man had a heart attack trying to help that cow. *Nee* one knew it. It turned into a blizzard and *nee* one found him until it melted. He and the cow both perished. I think of that every time it turns bitter and snows."

"That's horrible," Susan said with a shiver.

"We old timers always know things like that," Naomi said. "You live to be a certain age, you see a lot. Many times... Well, bad things can happen in life." She went back to working on the throw, but she looked like her thoughts were far away.

Ezra came in with a tray and mugs. "I thought I'd make hot chocolate for all of us. It tastes so *gut* when it's cold outside."

Naomi smiled. "*Denke*, Ezra. I would love a cup."

He set a cup on the small table beside her chair.

"Susan, I know I didn't ask if you wanted one, but I figured you did," he said and smiled.

"*Denke*," she said and took the offered cup. She inhaled the aroma wafting up from the cup. "It smells *wunderbaar*."

Ezra sat in the chair opposite Naomi and then scooted it closer to the wood stove. "This is kind of nice," he said. "The three of us staying warm and drinking hot chocolate."

Naomi nodded. "It is nice." She worked on the throw and sipped the hot chocolate.

Susan watched her covertly. Naomi was right about... just about everything. Hopefully, when she grew old, she'd have as much wisdom as Naomi. Maybe she hadn't been there with Naomi all that long, but she felt a closeness with the elder she hadn't expected.

Naomi was the kind of person who was just good for the soul. Her sweet and gentle nature was a salve that could remedy anything in Susan's world. Or at least that was what it seemed like. She felt like there was no problem she couldn't take to Naomi that the older woman wouldn't have good advice for.

As they sat companionably in the small parlor sipping chocolate and staying warm, the snow started coming down in earnest.

Susan fetched her Bible to read, and Ezra busied himself looking through a huge history book he'd found on Naomi's bookshelves.

Susan tried to concentrate on the Bible verses, but her mind kept coming back to how much she was enjoying their company. The kinship she felt in that little room was different from anything she'd ever felt before. She could have happily spent the next week without moving.

She didn't understand it, but she accepted it as fact.

She glanced out the window, and it was snowing even harder than it had been just a bit earlier. The windows were starting to get a bit of ice along the bottom of the panes, too. They were in for one bad storm unless she missed her guess.

Chapter Four

By the time evening came, the snow had accumulated until several inches blanketed the ground. But the more concerning part was that it was still snowing, and it was coming down furiously, to the point that it was difficult to see.

"I'm going with you to feed the animals," Ezra said. "I don't like this one bit. If it snows much harder, we won't be able to see where we're going. We need to run the cows into their shed and close them in, too."

Susan nodded. "We better go now, before it gets any worse. I have to take care of Nancy's animals, too."

"We'll do that as soon as we get ours taken care of," Ezra said.

They pulled on their boots and coats and hurried out into the freezing cold and snow. The snow came down so hard, Susan kept brushing it from her eyelashes. Their breath plumed out on the bitter-cold air.

They walked together to the barn, then Ezra went to get the cows into the shed, and she took care of feeding the other animals.

Susan practically ran to the pens to give the hungry animals feed and fresh water. By the time she finished, Ezra had brought in the cattle and given them their hay and feed. They had a water tank in the shed, so they didn't have to worry about carrying water.

"Let's take care of Nancy's animals so we can get back inside," she said.

They hurried next door and again divided up the work and took care of it as quickly as possible. Susan went to the house to check on Nancy and let her know the feeding was done. Then she ran to catch up with Ezra.

"Thanks for helping me," she said over the wind.

He grinned at her. "You're welcome. Let's get back to where it's warm and have some hot *kaffe*."

They raced back through the snow, laughing, and sliding until they got back to the house and scurried inside.

Naomi was in the kitchen. "I put *kaffe* on."

"*Wunderbaar*," Ezra said. "Does anyone want to play Timber King after supper?"

"*Jah*," Susan said. "I'll play."

"I will, too," Naomi said.

Susan loved playing board games. And what better time than when it was snowing so hard.

"I'm frying chicken for supper," Naomi said. "Susan, will you make the noodles and grate the cheese?"

"Of course. How about if we make cookies after supper?"

"I'm there for that," Ezra said. "I'll help make them."

Naomi smiled. "It's going to be a fun evening. I'll get the chicken started."

"Supper was delicious," Ezra said and patted his stomach.

Susan and Naomi had fixed it together.

"How much snow do you think we'll have by morning?" Susan asked.

Naomi had just started making cookie dough. "It hasn't let up all day. I'm guessing ten inches by morning at the least. I think it's going to be a blizzard by morning. You kids will have to be careful taking care of the animals."

"I hope it doesn't become a blizzard," Ezra said.

"I think it will be," Naomi said.

Susan and Ezra sat at the table while Naomi made the dough and cut out the first batch of cookies. Once they were in the oven, they played Timber King, and while more batches of cookies baked, they played Farm-opoly.

The baking and games went on past midnight until they were all yawning and laughing with each other.

Susan couldn't remember the last time she'd had so much fun.

When Susan got up early the next morning, snow still fell, and it was nearly impossible to see anything beyond a few feet out the windows. The wind howled like an angry beast battering the house.

She heard Naomi moving around in the parlor and then the kitchen.

Susan got dressed and went to help Naomi. She had just left her room when she heard a loud thud and Naomi cried out.

"Naomi?" Susan raced toward the kitchen. "Naomi, are you okay?"

"Susan! I've hurt myself."

Susan found Naomi on the kitchen floor where she'd fallen near the warming stove. Susan knelt beside her. "What happened? Are you hurt bad?"

"I've banged up my hip. I don't think it broke. But it hurts something awful. I don't know if I can get up yet," Naomi said.

Susan's heart pounded in her chest. What if Naomi had broken her hip and didn't realize it? What if she couldn't get up at all? What if they needed an ambulance?

"We need Ezra to help get you up," Susan said.

"I can get myself up, but I need to give it a couple of minutes." Naomi rubbed her hip and groaned.

"Are you sure it isn't broken?" Susan said.

"It hurts something awful, but I would be howling my head off if it was broken. I've known a couple women who broke a hip. I know what they said it was like."

Naomi pushed herself into a sitting position.

Ezra came hurrying into the kitchen. "*Grossmammi*, what happened? Are you hurt?"

"I've banged my hip up a bit. I don't think it broke. It sure hurts though. I guess you two can help me get up."

They each took one of her frail arms and gently pulled her up.

"*Ach, gut* heavens," Naomi said.

"Make sure she can stand before we let her go," Susan said.

"Let me see if I can walk on it," Naomi said and took a careful step. She nearly fell again. "I need a walking stick."

"Let's get you to the couch, and I'll go out and find you a walking stick," Ezra said.

"Don't go out in this storm. I have one, it was your grandfather's. It's behind the door in my bedroom."

"Let's get you to the couch," Susan said.

With one of them on each side of her, they supported her and very slowly, she walked to the couch and lowered herself.

"I'll go get the walking stick," Ezra said and went to fetch the stick. He returned a few minutes later with a walking stick with a carving of an old man in the handle.

"I remember this," Ezra said. "When I was little, I thought it had a scary old man inside the stick." He chuckled at himself.

"Don't worry about anything but resting your hip and letting it heal," Susan said. "I'll take care of everything."

Chapter Five

The snow continued for another twenty-four hours before it finally tapered off and stopped. Ezra helped with taking care of the animals. They churned through the deep snow, getting it down in their boots and chilling their feet. The temperature wasn't as blistering cold, but it was cold enough.

Susan had taken over all of the housework and cooking, so all Naomi had to do was concentrate on getting better. Susan provided her packs of ice from outdoors to place on her hip.

Naomi hated missing Sunday services, but they convinced her to stay home and not take a chance on aggravating her injury.

Susan and Ezra would go to church and come home as soon as the service was over so Susan could prepare lunch for all of them.

Susan pulled on her heaviest coat for the cold ride to the Bakers' home where services were being held that week. Ezra drove the buggy to the house and waited for her. She hurried out and climbed up beside him.

"It's still really cold," Ezra said.

"I know." Susan shivered inside her coat.

They rode slowly and carefully to the Bakers' and made their way down into the basement where the preaching service would be conducted. It was already crowded when they got there. The Bakers' basement wasn't as big as those in some of the other families' homes. But it would do.

They found their seating areas and Susan sat beside some of her friends.

Mary Brown, one of her best friends, leaned close and said, "Are you going to volunteer to help organize the youth Christmas dinner? They need extra people this year."

"I hadn't thought about it," Susan said. Maybe she should.

"You're *gut* at organizing and keeping things on track," Mary said. "Besides, it might be fun. I'm going to volunteer."

"Sure, I can help." There was no reason she shouldn't. Naomi had improved a little already. She would make a full recovery. Besides, it wouldn't take too much time in the planning meetings. Susan knew from past years, that planning meetings were never more than two hours at a time. And she could work on her own time at Naomi's. It sounded like a good opportunity to help the community.

As soon as services were over and announcements were made, Susan and Mary went to find the banquet planning chairwoman, Sadie Muller. They found her in the kitchen fixing a lunch plate.

"Hello, Mrs. Muller," Susan said. "Mary and I wanted to volunteer for the youth Christmas Banquet planning."

"*Gut*," Sadie said. "That makes four and including me, that's five."

"Who else is helping?" Mary said.

Sadie said, "Rebecca Harris and her boyfriend, Ezra Fisher. She lives in the next community."

Susan managed to keep an expressionless face. Well, this was going to be interesting. She'd never met Rebecca, and she had no desire to make her acquaintance. But it was too late to change her mind now.

Susan said, "I know Ezra. He's Widow Naomi's grandson."

"*Ach*, I didn't realize that's who he was," Sadie said.

"He's staying with us for a little while," Susan said. "He wants to fix her place up for her and spend time with her for the holidays."

Mary glanced over at Susan with widened eyes.

"That's *wunderbaar*," Sadie said. "I know Naomi must love having people with her. She's been alone so long."

"*Jah*, she was thrilled that he'd come to see her." How often did Naomi get company? No one other than Ezra had stopped by since she'd arrived. Of course, if Naomi requested help from the community, she would be flooded with people coming to help her out.

But she hadn't asked anything of anyone. While Naomi loved having company, she was fiercely independent.

"Where is Naomi?" Sadie said.

"She fell and bruised her hip," Susan said. "It still hurts too much for her to come outside."

"*Ach*, that don't sound *gut*," Sadie said.

"I better go find Ezra so I can get home and fix some lunch for Naomi."

"Let's fix her a nice plate here," Sadie said. "I saw some paper plates earlier." She rooted around in the supply cabinet until she found one. "Here we go. Let's give her some chicken. I know she loves that."

Sadie piled on roasted chicken, macaroni and cheese, potato salad, and green beans, and then covered the food with foil. "Now you won't have to cook the moment you get home."

"*Denke*," Susan said. "She'll love it, too. She'll know she was thought about."

Sadie nodded. "I should speak with some of the ladies about visiting her."

"That would be nice," Susan said. "She would appreciate it."

Did Naomi think people didn't care because no one came to visit with her? She hoped not. Naomi was a sweet elder who deserved to know she was loved. But no one had been there since Susan had arrived weeks before.

Of course, Naomi saw people at Sunday services. Still, it would be nice if someone stopped by every now and then.

"*Denke* for volunteering," Sadie said bringing the conversation back to the banquet. "I was starting to think the three of us were going to have to do everything by ourselves. Our first meeting is this Thursday at two o'clock at the library, in the back meeting room. I've reserved it for all the meetings. Same time, every Thursday, until the banquet dinner."

"We'll be there," Susan said. "I'm looking forward to helping out." Already some ideas were popping up. They would have a wonderful Christmas banquet for the district's youth.

Susan and Mary left the kitchen to find Ezra.

"I can't believe Ezra is staying with you and Naomi," Mary said. "He's so cute."

"He's also dating someone. And I'm not interested in him," Susan said.

"That's too bad," Mary said. "But *jah*, he's off limits, I s'pose."

"It's nothing to me," Susan said. "I'm not interested in him. He's fun to talk to and play board games with. And he helps me take care of the animals. But he isn't the right kind of man for me."

"*Ach*, he's the right kind of man for any woman," Mary said and laughed.

Susan joined her.

"I better go look for my folks," Mary said.

"Okay," Susan said. "I'll see you at the meeting."

She went to find Ezra so they could get back to Naomi's. She didn't want to leave Naomi alone any longer than necessary. She found him in the parlor sharing a plate with a pretty girl with ash-blonde hair. That had to be Rebecca. She was tall and thin. Ezra said something, and she laughed in a light and airy tone, like she didn't have a care in the world.

Ezra stared at her like a love-sick puppy.

Susan wanted to turn around and leave, but she couldn't. They needed to get back and make sure Naomi was okay. At least they had a nice lunch already prepared for Naomi; she would be hungry by the time they got home.

"Ezra," she said, "I need to get back to Naomi's place. She'll be hungry, and she shouldn't be trying to fix herself some food."

He looked apologetically at Rebecca. "We must leave. Susan's right, I don't want my *Grossmammi* getting hurt again."

Rebecca looked annoyed, but said, "Of course. You can't take a chance with something like that."

"Rebecca, this is Susan, I told you about her."

Rebecca nodded. "*Jah*, I remember. Nice to meet you, Susan."

"It's nice to meet you, too," Susan said.

She couldn't help but notice that Rebecca didn't look very happy to meet her. Well, that was her business. Wait until she found out she and Mary had volunteered to organize the banquet with her.

Chapter Six

By Thursday, some of the snow had melted off. The temperature had risen enough that by the time Susan and Ezra were ready to go to the Christmas banquet meeting, she was eager to be on their way.

Ezra harnessed his horse and picked up Susan at the house.

By now Naomi was doing better, though she still had pain and limped. But she was in good spirits. Susan enjoyed looking after her and cooking for all of them. Ezra and Naomi seemed to be enjoying the time they were spending together.

It seemed strange to look back and recall how reluctant she had been to spend the winter with Naomi. Now it was more like being with another part of her family.

Ezra's horse trotted at a brisk clip toward town, and they reached the library quicker than she expected. He helped her out of the buggy, and they hurried inside the library. She knew where the meeting room was in the back of the library.

When they went inside, Sadie and Rebecca were already there waiting for them.

"Ah, you're here," Sadie said.

Rebecca smiled at Ezra, and he grinned and went to her.

Mary hurried in a moment later.

"We're all here," Sadie said and smiled. "*Denke* for coming. This is our first meeting. And the first things we need to talk about are where we're going to hold the banquet and how we'll decorate. The Weiss *familye* has offered to host the event. Their home is one of the biggest in the community, and it's among the favored places for church services because their basement is warm and big enough to hold everyone without being cramped."

"It's absolutely the best option," Susan said.

"We could find a place in town," Rebecca said. "That way we wouldn't have to be in a dark basement."

"Their basement isn't dark," Susan said. "It's very clean, and it's painted white."

"Still," Rebecca said, "it's a basement." She looked displeased.

Susan inhaled deeply. "Other than an absence of windows, it's no different than the ground floor of the home. It's nice down there."

"I can't justify renting, when we have a perfectly *gut* offer of a home," Sadie said. "It would cost a lot of money to rent a hall for one night. That money can be better spent helping members of our community who need it. We have a high elder population and a lot of widows. I'd rather see that money go to help them."

"I agree," Susan said.

Rebecca grudgingly nodded.

"I think it only makes sense to take the offer for the *haus*," Mary said.

"All right. We agree on the *haus*," Sadie said. "Now moving on to getting the decorations ready. Before our next meeting, we should all write out some ideas on decorating and activities our youth can participate in."

Sadie reached inside a large bag she'd brought along. "I have a bunch of folders. You can all have one or two to keep track of anything you want to bring to meetings." She handed out a stack of folders to each of them.

As the meeting progressed, Rebecca seemed to have something against everything anyone else suggested. Why had she volunteered in the first place? It appeared she'd mistaken the volunteer job for some kind of debating activity.

Susan and Mary exchanged glances a couple of times.

Susan looked at Ezra who looked annoyed every time Rebecca went on a litany of complaints.

By the end of the meeting, Susan couldn't wait to get back to Naomi's and have a cup of coffee. The meeting had been exhausting because of Rebecca's constant disagreements with everything anyone suggested.

Susan went to the front of the library with Mary to give Ezra a little time with Rebecca. The situation was a little awkward with her having to ride home with the other girl's boyfriend. She was certain Rebecca didn't like it.

And if she were going to be honest, she couldn't blame Rebecca. It had to be...well, she wasn't certain what Rebecca was thinking, but she couldn't be happy that her boyfriend was staying under the same roof with another woman.

At least in that respect, she couldn't find fault with any objections Rebecca might have.

While they waited, her thoughts turned to Christmas and gift giving. She typically knitted or crocheted things for people. Naomi was easy enough, she would make a nice lap throw for her. But what should she make for Ezra? Maybe a nice scarf and matching knitted hat? Yes, that would be nice.

Finally, Ezra and Rebecca came to the front of the library, and Susan's stomach knotted. She paused. Why was the reappearance of Rebecca putting her on edge? And she was definitely on edge. Her good humor had vanished the moment Rebecca came into the same section of the library.

She glanced at Ezra and then at Rebecca, and an awful realization closed over her. She was starting to have feelings for Ezra.

The rest of the week followed the pattern that had become familiar. Susan took care of the household chores and cooking while Naomi took it easy and rested her hip, though she had insisted on baking. Susan stayed in the kitchen with her and put Naomi's creations in the oven and then took them out for her.

She and Ezra continued to care for Naomi's and Nancy's animals. They had it down to a routine, working together, yet competing to see who could get the most done the quickest.

That morning, when Susan went to tell Nancy that her animals were fed and well, Nancy's eyes were red from crying.

"Nancy, what's wrong? Is you *boppli* okay?"

Nancy nodded and produced a sickly-looking smile. "I'm just so lonely, and this morning the table leg came off, and I can't fix it."

She looked like she was going to cry again.

Susan caught her hands. "I want you to gather up Ivan and come over to Naomi's house. We'll have some *kaffe* and pie and chat. I'm sure Ezra and I can fix your table, too." Susan felt terrible that she hadn't thought about Nancy all alone with only a newborn for company.

"Are you sure Naomi won't mind?" Nancy said.

"I'm sure," Susan said.

Nancy smiled. "I would love that."

"Then get Ivan ready, and let's go.

It didn't take Nancy long to get her son ready, and they hurried over to Naomi's house and entered through the back door into the kitchen.

The baby was still sleepy despite being out in the cold air for a few minutes.

"We need somewhere safe for Ivan to sleep," Susan said. "I know, we have a big basket we could let him sleep in close to the stove. I'll go get it."

By the time Susan returned with a large basket and a blanket folded up in the bottom for a cushion, Nancy had taken Ivan's coat off. She snuggled Ivan into the basket and covered him with the blanket she'd wrapped around his coat.

He cooed as he drifted off to sleep.

"I'm glad you came over," Susan said. "I'll make some *kaffe*. We have a nice pumpkin pie. We can have some of that, too. But first I want to tell Naomi we have company."

"All right," Nancy said.

Susan went to the parlor where Naomi was working on a quilt square and Ezra was reading a geography book.

"Nancy came over for a visit. She was lonely and crying, and I asked her to come over. Ezra, the leg broke off her table. I told her we could probably fix it for her."

"Sure," Ezra said. "It's likely an easy repair."

Naomi stood. "Let's all go to the kitchen and have a *gut* visit with her." Naomi appeared to be feeling spry. But Susan stuck close by her for the walk to the kitchen.

"Nancy, it's so *gut* to see you," Naomi said.

"*Gut* to see you, too, Miss Naomi. I was feeling cooped up, so it's nice to get out for a while."

"You're welcome to come over any time," Naomi said. "I love having company."

"*Denke*. You can't imagine how much I appreciate that. It's been a long time since my husband left. I had *nee* idea he'd have work so late in the year."

"Do you have plans for Thanksgiving next week?" Naomi said.

"*Nee.* I don't." She looked hopeful.

"Then come over here for dinner with us," Naomi said.

"I'd love that," she said. "*Denke* for the invitation."

"Come any time," Naomi said.

"It's nice to know we won't spend Thanksgiving alone," she said.

Again, Susan felt terrible that she hadn't realized Nancy was so lonely. She always tapped on the door to let Nancy know the animals had been cared for. Nancy always asked if she wanted to come in, but she was always rushing to get all her chores done. It hadn't occurred to her that Nancy was practically begging for someone to talk to.

She would make it a point to stop in at least for a cup of coffee. It bothered her that she had been so wrapped up in thinking about the banquet, her chores...and Ezra, that she'd failed to notice someone in need when they were right in front of her.

She needed to pray over it and ask for guidance and help regarding being able to see when someone needed her.

Naomi stood carefully. "I think the *kaffe* is ready, and we have pumpkin pies. I think there's some vanilla ice cream in the freezer if you'd like some."

Naomi was still using her walking stick, so she moved carefully to the stove.

"I would love a piece of pie," Nancy said. She smiled and it lit up her entire face.

Susan felt like kicking herself. She had to do better. And she needed to keep her mind off Ezra.

Chapter Seven

The library buzzed with activity when Susan and Ezra arrived for the second banquet planning meeting.

Once again, Sadie and Mary were already there, and Rebecca had also just arrived. Rebecca hung up her coat and took a seat in the middle of the table, forcing Ezra to sit on one side of her and Susan on the other.

Susan was pretty sure she'd done it on purpose.

Did Rebecca think she was spending too much time with Ezra? Maybe she was. She supposed she couldn't be too annoyed with the girl.

Susan didn't have any hard feelings toward the young woman. Rebecca had every right to be concerned when she knew they were living under the same roof. And she didn't even know Susan had feelings where Ezra was concerned. But Rebecca honestly had nothing to worry about. Susan would never consider trying to take someone else's boyfriend.

That was not the action of a God-fearing woman. And not something she wanted to be involved with. There was no honor in stealing a boyfriend.

"I'm afraid I have bad news," Sadie said. "The offer to use the basement has been taken back. It appears there's a problem with a leak and they've had to bring in some help to repair the damage. The work won't be done in time for the dinner."

Rebecca looked as if she was trying hard not to smile.

"We will be renting the hall in town," Sadie said. "We don't have any other options on such short notice."

"I'm sure this will work better for us," Rebecca said.

"Honestly, it probably will," Sadie said. "I wanted to save the money for other things. But the youth dinner is important, too. So, that's our decision at this point."

Rebecca had several folders, presumably of ideas and maybe drawings of her ideas. Susan had brought several folders as well. She set them beside her. Rebecca could share her information first.

Rebecca was more than happy to show the work she'd done. She went through each piece of paper and discussed each point without even considering that maybe not all of them would agree they were all good ideas.

"So," Rebecca said, "I think we should have candles and poinsettias on each table at four-foot intervals. The tables will be long enough to have at least three arrangements per table."

"I don't know," Susan said. "I really don't know about having burning candles on the tables. I was thinking lanterns might give a nice touch. They put out more light, too. Maybe we could use the candles on the dessert table."

Rebecca stuck out her lip. "It won't look as nice with lanterns."

"Hmmm," Sadie said. "I think they will be just as pretty. And I know they give more light. We can leave the poinsettias on the tables. Those are beautiful, and we won't have to worry about the candles falling over."

"Okay, fine," Rebecca said. "What about entertainment?"

"We should have some games," Susan said.

"I agree," Mary said.

"I think we should have blindfold giftwrapping for the younger youth," Susan said. "It would be fun for everyone even if they don't participate."

"What is that?" Ezra said.

"You have someone try to wrap a box while they wear a blindfold. Everyone makes a mess, and everyone has fun watching them try."

"I say *jah*," Mary said.

"Me too," Sadie said. "The younger youth would probably love that."

The meeting stretched out until everyone had presented their ideas.

"We're coming along well," Sadie said. "I want everyone to keep thinking of ideas. I've already requested the hall, so we've secured that. I'll place an order for the poinsettias this week. We should start making paper snowflakes to hang. We'll need lots of them. So, the more the merrier. And with that, I say we call this meeting over."

Susan said, "Agreed."

Rebecca didn't look completely happy, but she nodded. Mary and Ezra both nodded as well.

Rebecca started gathering up her folders. "We've got our folders mixed together."

"Here, I'll help you," Susan said.

"*Nee*," Rebecca snapped. "I've got it."

"Okay then." Susan exchanged a glance with Mary.

"Here," Rebecca said. "These are yours." She pushed a stack of folders toward Susan.

"*Denke*," Susan said. She tucked them back into her bag. "Ezra, I'll be out front whenever you're ready to go home."

She didn't wait for him to respond. She headed out with Mary right behind her. She didn't want to ruffle Rebecca's feathers any more than she already had. It wasn't her fault Rebecca's idea of candles had been overruled.

Well, there was nothing she could do about it. Maybe she could find some way to assuage Rebecca's feelings. She had no desire to upset her. She walked with Mary to the front of the library, and they sat on a bench to wait for Ezra.

"Rebecca really wanted those candles," Mary said.

"I know. I just like more light when I'm eating. And they could tip over."

"You don't have to explain it to me," Mary said.

"I know. Although, I feel kind of bad about it now." She rubbed her forehead.

Ezra and Rebecca walked out together. Rebecca looked annoyed. The two of them stopped and spoke quietly, then Rebecca walked away from the library with her head held higher than usual.

Ezra hurried over to them. "I guess we'd better go. Mary, do you need a ride home?"

"*Nee*," Mary said. "My *bruder's* picking me up. He's probably almost here."

"Okay. If you ever need a ride home from the meetings, just let us know."

"Thanks," Mary said. "I appreciate that." Mary turned her head. "There he is. I'll see you guys at church."

"See you," Susan said.

Mary waved and hurried toward her brother's buggy.

Susan and Ezra climbed into his buggy and headed for home at a brisk trot.

"There's a blanket behind the seat, if you're cold," Ezra said.

"I'm fine. But thanks. If I get cold, I'll grab it," she said.

He smiled and nodded.

Why did he have to be so handsome? It would be easier to ignore him if he had ordinary looks. But he didn't. And she caught herself looking at him much too often. Not only that, but she'd also caught herself thinking Rebecca was a lucky woman. She shouldn't be thinking about him at all.

She studied the snow-covered fields to avoid looking in his direction. Patches of brown grass stood tall here and there. And a red barn stood out against the gray horizon. Cows stood in the ankle-deep snow as if they didn't even mind.

"What are you looking at so intently?" he asked.

"Just the landscape," she said. "Everything is so pretty all covered in snow."

"*Jah*, it is," he said. "I've always loved winter. Most people look forward to spring. But I look forward to winter. I guess I'm strange."

"I don't think you're strange at all," she said. "I don't love the cold. But winter is necessary for the earth to prepare for the next season. And it is beautiful."

"I'm glad you don't think I'm strange," he said. Their gazes met, and his lips quirked up in a smile that nearly melted her heart.

Then he grinned as if realizing how she'd reacted to him.

They needed to get home so she wasn't in such close proximity to him. He had a beautiful girlfriend. They shouldn't be looking at each other like this. It was all wrong.

He was suddenly in a hurry to get home, and she understood why he wanted to spend time as much time as possible with his grandmother. Naomi was getting up in years, and she was frail. Susan didn't want to think of all the things that could happen to the older woman.

In the short time she'd been there, she'd become very fond of Naomi. Susan knew without a doubt that she would visit Naomi and help her out for the rest of her life. She didn't understand why more people didn't come visit more often.

She was thrilled Nancy had come over the other day and would continue to come over and visit. God had surely wanted the two women to meet and help each other stave off loneliness for one another.

Finally, they pulled into the driveway, and he stopped at the house to let her out while he took care of the horse.

She grabbed her bag and jumped down.

He drove to the barn, and she went inside the house, glad for the warmth that enveloped her. Naomi sat in the kitchen with a large cup of coffee and a brownie.

"I made a batch of brownies while you were gone," she said. "They're delicious. You'd better grab a couple before Ezra gets in here and sees them." She chuckled.

"I think I will," Susan said and cut one out of the pan.

"I'm telling you," Naomi said. "You better take another. That boy is like a ravenous wolf."

Susan laughed. "Okay, I'll take one more." She cut another one and put both on a napkin. "I'm going to take my things to my room. I'll be back in a few minutes."

Naomi nodded.

Susan hurried to her room and set everything down so she could remove her coat and hang it up.

She pulled out the folders and took the top one and sat on the bed. She grabbed one of the brownies and took a bite. It was delicious.

She opened the folder and looked at the top page. It wasn't hers.

What?

It must be Rebecca's folder. She went to place the paper back in the folder and her gaze landed on the paper that had been under the one she held. It was a letter. She didn't intend to read it, but she saw the salutation and stopped cold. It read *My Dearest David*.

David? Was she writing to some other man? Or was this business?

She picked up the paper. She shouldn't read it. It was not for her. But was Rebecca cheating on Ezra? She bit her lip. It wasn't her place to read this. Yet if she didn't, she would always wonder if Rebecca was doing him wrong.

She sat down with the letter and began reading.

By the time she finished, she was angry. She glanced through the folder and found two more letters. There were also four letters to her from the mysterious David. Clearly, they were carrying on a tryst through the mail.

And Ezra had no idea. Her stomach churned. Should she tell him?

She didn't want to be responsible for breaking them up; that wouldn't sit right with her. But if she didn't say something, he might continue to pursue an unfaithful woman. And that wouldn't sit right with her either.

What should she do? Could she talk to Naomi? No. Because she would turn around and tell Ezra which would be the same as if she told him herself.

She bit her lip. She didn't know what to do, and she couldn't talk to anyone about it.

Chapter Eight

Ezra took a long drink of hot coffee and covertly watched Susan as she finished breakfast. He glanced over at his grandmother, and she was blatantly watching him.

He glanced away.

He didn't know what was going on with Susan, but something wasn't right. She'd been unusually quiet for the last two days, and she seemed distracted. She couldn't seem to keep her mind on anything since they'd come home from the banquet planning meeting.

He'd racked his brain trying to remember if anything had seemed off at the meeting. Rebecca had been argumentative, but that hadn't seemed to bother Susan.

Nothing had happened at the meeting. Something had occurred after they got home. Maybe he should try to talk to his grandmother. She might know something. If she knew what was going on, maybe he could get her to tell him because he was having no luck with Susan.

He'd tried talking to her several times, but she'd made excuses to go do something else. Whatever was going on, he was determined to get to the bottom of it before the day was out.

They were still feeding the animals together, though she always stopped in to see how Nancy was doing every morning. Had she maybe told Nancy what was bothering her?

It didn't matter; he couldn't go ask her with her husband away from home. It didn't feel appropriate to him. It might even scare her, and he didn't want that. He didn't know her well enough to approach her at church and start asking questions either.

So, he would just have to wonder about it if he couldn't get Susan to tell him what was going on. But he didn't plan on that. He was going to find out one way or another. And the best approach would probably be just to say he knew something was wrong, and he wasn't going to let it go.

That was his plan to get her to talk. And this was as good a day as any to put it into action.

But if his grandmother knew what was troubling Susan,

maybe she would tell him, and he wouldn't have to confront Susan.

Susan served up a breakfast of eggs, ham, and fried potatoes.

"Susan, you're an excellent cook," he said. He meant it, too.

Her cheeks pinked up a little. "*Denke*," she said with a little smile.

"You're welcome."

His grandmother was looking at him again. He lifted one eyebrow in question. She just smiled and picked up her fork. Did she know something he didn't? It sure seemed like she had opinions on something at the very least.

"Do either of you need anything from town?" he asked in a casual tone. "I'm driving in for a couple of things."

"Well," his grandmother said, "I'm sure I can think of an item or two if you're going to stop at the mercantile."

"I am," he said. "Just let me know what you want, and I'll pick it up for you."

"I'll make a small list," she said. "As long as you don't mind."

"I don't mind at all. I'll pick up half the items in the store if you need them."

She laughed. "It isn't that big of a list."

He turned to Susan. "How about you? Would you like to ride along with me?"

She hesitated a moment, then said, "*Jah*, I could use a couple of things. And I can help get Naomi's things at the mercantile."

"*Gut*. We'll leave later this morning. Hopefully, it'll warm up a little more before we leave."

By the time Ezra got his horse hitched up and they were ready to go, it was already past noon and they'd eaten a quick lunch. He didn't mind though as it had warmed up a bit over the last few hours.

He helped Susan into the buggy, and he climbed up beside her and picked up the reins.

"Ready?" he said.

"Indeed, I am."

"All right then," he said and clucked to the horse who trotted off down the driveway and turned onto the main road.

He stewed over exactly what he wanted to say until he realized they were more than halfway to town. He needed to get on with it. He rehearsed it in his head for a few moments then said, "I know something's wrong. You've been acting strangely since the meeting, and I want to know if I did something to offend you or if it's something else. I'm not going to drop this until you tell me the truth."

She squirmed and looked across the open field. She glanced at him then looked away again.

"You have to tell me," he said. "You can't get away from this when we live under the same roof."

She sighed and rubbed her forehead. "You have done nothing wrong."

"Then what is it?" He was starting to feel a little annoyed. Why wouldn't she tell him?

"I found out something by accident," she said. She spoke slowly as if picking her way through a street full of potholes.

"I don't understand," he said.

"I know. I'm sorry." She bit her lip.

"This is obviously distressing you. Therefore, it must be something of a significant weight. If it involves me, you have *nee* right to keep it from me." Something was definitely going on. And he needed to know what it was.

"You're right," she said. "Look, I didn't know what to do when I found out. I didn't want to be in the middle of something that was none of my business. In truth, I went too far into it as it is."

"What do you mean? Something had to have happened at the meeting that I didn't realize. It's the only thing that makes sense."

She nodded and looked away.

"Tell, me. You must," he said.

"At the meeting, we all had the same kind of folders. Sadie gave them to us. Anyway, I had some scattered on the table and so did Rebecca."

What in the world did the folders have to do with it? He was still confused.

"When we left, Rebecca and I gathered up our folders. When I got home, I was going to look at the drawings and ideas I had. Except, I had one of Rebecca's folders. I didn't know it until I opened it."

His heart thudded in his chest. She'd found something in that folder. Something that related to him. "What did you find?"

"Are you sure you want to know?" She met his gaze head on.

Without hesitation, he said, "*Jah*."

"I saw a letter addressed to someone called David. I shouldn't have read it. But I did. Because the first thing I thought was that she was carrying on with another man."

"And?" he said

"She is. There were letters from him to her as well. I didn't read those. But I'm sorry." She didn't know what else to say. He'd insisted she tell him. She felt awful about it, but what was she supposed to do when he'd insisted?

"I see," he said slowly. "I... I had *nee* idea. But I should have guessed something was going on. She'd been acting a little differently for a while. I guess she's trying to figure out which one of us she wants to continue with."

"Well, she's a fool if she doesn't pick you," Susan blurted. Heat filled her cheeks, and she glanced away. Dear Lord—how could she had said it like that? Hopefully, he hadn't noticed. She turned back, and he was looking at her with his head slightly tilted.

"*Denke*," he said, "for letting me know." His voice sounded strained, and he looked straight ahead. "I appreciate it more than you know."

Chapter Nine

Ezra wasn't looking forward to seeing Rebecca. He suspected it wasn't going to be pleasant. His breath puffed out as white vapor, just like his horse's breath as they trotted along the roadway.

Fresh snow blanketed the asphalt, muffling the horse's hoof beats. And the harness rings jingled merrily as the horse whisked the buggy along the snow-covered surface.

Normally, he would have waited for better weather to go to her parents' house, but this wouldn't wait. He had to know what she had to say for herself. There wasn't a doubt in his mind what Susan had said was true. Besides, she'd asked if he wanted to see the letters. He'd declined.

He wished he could say he was shocked, but he wasn't.

What had surprised him was Susan's off-hand remark that Rebecca would be a fool if she didn't pick him. What had she mean by that? Was she interested in him? Or was she just being nice and maybe didn't want him to feel any worse about what Rebecca was doing?

He wished he knew how she really felt about it. But he wasn't going to guess and perhaps look like a big fool.

He tried to push it all from his mind for the rest of the drive which was a good thirty minutes. He was it dreading the upcoming conversation with Rebecca. But, at the same time, he seemed to be looking forward to it.

He stopped his horse near their porch and hurried from the buggy to the door. He rapped on the frame, and a few moments later, Rebecca's mother answered.

"Ezra, how nice to see you. Come one in."

"It's nice to see you, too," he said as he stepped inside.

"Rebecca's in the parlor reading. Go on in. She'll be glad to see you."

"*Denke*," he said. He wasn't sure about that at all.

He walked through the house he had become familiar with over the last several months to the parlor. Rebecca sat beside the tall window with a paperback book. She was so engrossed in the book she didn't realize he was there.

"Hello, Rebecca," he said.

She jumped and let out a little yelp of surprise. "Ezra, I didn't hear you. What are you doing here today?"

"I came to talk to you about something important," he said.

"*Ach*." She looked surprised. "What's that?"

He glanced around to make sure they were alone, and then he spoke in a quiet voice. "It's about the letters going between you and David." He intently watched her expression change from her usual self to a guarded look.

"Excuse me?" she said. "I'm afraid I don't know what you mean."

He pushed his hair back off his forehead. "I think you know exactly what I mean. *Nee*. I don't think it. I *know* it. I know about the letters to and from David. So don't bother pretending you don't know what I'm talking about, because you do."

"Fine," she said. "I was exchanging letters with someone from another community. It wasn't anything serious."

"It's serious enough for me. You were writing to another *mann* behind my back. And you knew I wouldn't be okay with it, or you would have told me." He didn't know if he was more angry or more hurt.

"So, what do you want me to say?"

"Nothing. Absolutely nothing," he said, and he couldn't hide the disgust in his voice.

"What are *you* saying?" she said.

"That we're finished." He didn't give her time to respond. He turned and walked out.

He hurried out of the house and got into his buggy.

The drive back to his grandmother's was cold, both the weather and his heart. He still couldn't believe Rebecca had been so casual about it, but she had. Now he wasn't sure if he'd ever really known her at all.

He'd never suspected she was doing something like that.

With the cold biting into him, he was glad to turn into his grandmother's driveway. He drove to the barn and took care of his horse. At least, it was warmer in the barn with all the animals stabled inside.

After making sure his horse was comfortable, he hurried to the house. He found Susan in the kitchen preparing to put icing on a chocolate cake.

"You look half-frozen," she said. "I'll make some hot *kaffe* and warm you up."

He pulled out a chair and sat. "Thanks, I'd appreciate that."

She got the coffee brewing and then went to finish slathering icing on the cake. "We can have a slice of cake with the *kaffe*."

"Sounds great," he said. In truth, it sounded better than great. Anything she baked was guaranteed to be delicious.

"What's wrong? You seem...not yourself."

He let out a sigh. "I went to confront Rebecca."

"*Ach, nee*," she said. "Should I ask how it went?"

"She denied it, and I told her I knew she was lying. In the end, I told her we were finished. I mean, how could she have expected anything else?" It felt good to have it said and done.

"I'm really sorry," Susan said. "That must have been difficult. If there's anything I can do to help..."

"Don't be sorry. I'm not. Not truly. I would much rather know now before this went any further. I could never marry a woman who was dishonest about something like that."

Who knew what else she'd lied about? He would never know.

Susan smoothed on more icing. "I suppose you're right."

"I know I'm right," he said. "If she'd lied about that, she's lied about other things as well."

"Still, I'm sorry. It had to be tough to go through," she said.

"I s'pose. *Jah*. It was. But I feel better now," he said. "It's time to continue on."

"I suppose there isn't any other choice," she said softly.

He met her gaze and held it. "There isn't. It's finished with her."

What was she thinking? He wished he knew. Susan would never date someone while writing to someone else on the side. She was loyal. He'd been around her long enough to know what she was like.

She was beautiful, faithful, hardworking, and kind. The sort of person it was a pleasure to be around. Susan was an absolute angel in watching out for his grandmother. He didn't know what his grandmother would have done without her.

She was...

What exactly was he doing? What was happening? Did he have feelings for Susan?

Chapter Ten

Susan put two pans of dough into the oven and checked the fire. Soon the kitchen would be filled with the delicious aroma of baking bread. It was one of the things she liked best. And it would taste even better than it smelled with a little wood smoke from the fire.

Naomi sat at the table working on a piece of embroidery.

That week the temperature dropped again, and bitter cold wind crept around the house. But the kitchen stayed warm all day because either Susan or Naomi was baking or cooking something.

The scent of fresh coffee lingered in the air. Susan breathed it in, taking pleasure in the aroma. Ezra had carried in load after load of wood for Naomi.

Susan did all the housework and most of the cooking. She'd taken over running the house, so Naomi didn't have to do anything but continue to recover. And even now that she was much better, Susan kept doing most of the work. She wanted to make life as easy and pleasant for Naomi as possible.

Ezra had been fixing everything that needed repairs in Naomi's house. He had been a real godsend. While Naomi's home wasn't in bad shape, it had reached a point where it needed some things taken care of so they wouldn't become worse.

The wind cut loose again, buffeting at the house with a vengeance.

"That's a wicked wind," Naomi said as she stitched a piece of cloth that would eventually become part of a quilt block.

Susan poured herself a cup of coffee. "Would you like another cup?" she asked Naomi.

"*Nee*, dear. I'm fine. I still have a little left."

Ezra came in and brushed snow from his sleeves. "It's starting to snow again."

Susan glanced out the window and sure enough, snow had started falling again.

Naomi finished her coffee and pushed her chair back. "If you *kinner* don't mind, I'm going to go to the parlor and read for a while. A little smile curled the corner of her lips.

"I think I'm going to bake a peach cobbler," Susan said.

"Why don't you make two and take one over to Nancy when you do the evening feeding?" Naomi said.

Susan nodded. "I will. I know she bakes a lot, too. But I'm sure she would love that."

Naomi nodded and left for the parlor. Ezra sat at the table and leaned back in the chair.

"Would you like some *kaffe*?" she asked. "It's still fresh."

"I'd love a cup."

She grabbed a heavy mug, filled it, and took it to him. She picked up the sugar and cream and set them on the table.

He stirred sugar and cream into the coffee. "*Denke*."

"You're welcome," she said. She enjoyed doing little things for him.

"You're a *gut* cook. And baker," he said.

"*Denke*." She smiled at him. His compliments always sounded so sincere, and she appreciated them all the more because of it.

"I love to cook," she said. "I like preserving food, too." She chuckled lightly. "Some of my best memories are of *Mamm* and me canning and putting up food in the freezer."

"Sounds *gut* to me," he said.

She sat down at the table across from him. "I remember one time when things didn't go as we planned. We made this huge crock full of sauerkraut. The batch went bad. And when we got up the next morning, the house was full of flies."

He laughed. "*Ach*, I got an image of that in my head because I know sauerkraut smells awful if it goes over. And I can see that happening."

"We swatted flies all day and opened the door and kitchen windows to try to shoo them away. But we got more in the *haus*," she said. "It was awful." And then she laughed, too. She couldn't stop herself.

"We haven't made a batch of sauerkraut since that happened," she said.

He grinned. "Well, you might not have gotten what you set out to make, but you ended up with a funny story."

"What about you?" she said. "Do you have any funny stories?"

He hesitated. "I shouldn't tell this, but it's the funniest and most embarrassing thing that's ever happened to me."

"You have to tell it now," she said, beyond intrigued.

"Okay, I'll tell, but I'm going to be embarrassed," he said. "This happened four years ago, when I was sixteen. I went with some friends of mine to a swimming hole we'd heard about, but we'd never gone to before. It was far away, but we walked instead of taking a buggy."

"I'm guessing that was your first mistake?" she said.

"You'd be guessing right," he said and gave her a lopsided grin.

"Tell me," she said and giggled.

"So, we walked to the swimming hole, and it took more than an hour to get there. None of us had swim trunks. We got the bright idea to go swimming when we got there. We weren't too concerned about not having swimming clothes."

"*Ach nee*," she said. "This is going somewhere bad."

"*Jah*, it is," he said. "There was absolutely no one else around. So we stripped off our clothes and hung them on bushes. Then we ran for the water and jumped in. It was gloriously cold, and we had the best time that afternoon. But eventually, we decided we'd better head for home. So, we got out of the water and went for our clothes. And they were all gone."

"What?" She bit her lip to keep from laughing.

"Gone. Just vanished while we were playing around in the water. We didn't see anyone. But someone was there. And that someone took all our clothes."

She now clapped a hand over her mouth to try to stop the giggles.

"So, we had *nee* choice and *nee* clothes. We had to walk home completely naked. We broke off branches to cover ourselves the best we could, and we stayed off the roads as much as we could. We walked through brush and brambles. Over rocks.

Sometimes we had to walk on the road and every time we heard a car or saw a buggy in the distance, we ran off the road and either had to find a place to hide or we laid on the ground and hoped *nee* one saw us. By the time we got home, we were a mess."

She couldn't stop giggling. "I know it wasn't funny. But it is funny to hear about."

"*Jah*, it was horrible. And you know what?"

"What?" she said.

"Whoever the prankster was must have thought they were truly funny, because the next day, I found my clothes scattered across the front lawn. The others found their clothes in their yards, too. Someone thought they were being clever."

"I can't even imagine something like that happening," she said. "But at least they returned your clothes."

"I can't imagine it either, and I was there," he said and laughed. "That was probably inappropriate for me to share, but that's the funniest and most awful thing that has happened to me."

The following day was carried in by the blustering winds, and Susan and Ezra took care of the animals as quickly as they could. They had their routine down, and they each did their part and scrambled back to the house and the warmth inside.

She made fresh coffee to warm them up.

Susan was probably enjoying her time with Ezra much more than she should. But she didn't care. There was nothing that could take away her good humor. She spent the rest of the morning dusting and tidying up for Naomi who sat in the parlor reading their local Amish paper.

Susan had finished her chores and gone to the kitchen to prepare lunch when a knock sounded on the front door.

"Ezra, could you get that? I'm trying to get our lunch in the oven," she called to him.

"Sure," he called back and a moment later she heard the door open.

"Rebecca? What are you doing here?" Ezra asked.

Rebecca? Why was she here? From what Susan had heard, Rebecca had gone to help take care of a cousin's newborn baby. She wasn't due back in town yet. From the kitchen, Susan could hear what she had to say.

"Can we talk for just a minute?" Rebecca said.

Ezra spoke with weariness in his voice. "I really don't—"

"Please, just give me five minutes. Come out to my buggy," Rebecca said.

"Well—"

"Please," she said.

"All right."

Susan's stomach tightened into a painful knot. Why was he going to talk to her? Hadn't he learned anything about her? Susan had a bad feeling. Only one thing had brought Rebecca to Naomi's. And it wasn't to see how Naomi was doing. She'd come to try to coax Ezra back to her.

Well, if he fell for it, then he wasn't as smart as she thought he was. She restrained herself from childishly stomping her foot. She'd thought that maybe something was developing between her and Ezra. Had she been wrong? She didn't want to think so. But if that was true, would he have gone outside to talk with Rebecca?

Susan didn't want to think he would take her back, but she feared his good nature might overrule common sense.

Chapter Eleven

Susan was not looking forward to the Christmas banquet planning meeting.

She had no idea what had happened between Ezra and Rebecca the day she'd come to Naomi's. Ezra had remained quiet about it, and Susan would never ask. But he had been spending more time to himself, so it didn't seem he had any interest in Susan.

In turn, she felt rejected and unhappy when he was around her. They did the chores together as always, but it had changed from enjoying light banter while they worked to a situation where they hardly spoke. It was as if each of them was lost in deep thought and nothing else made it through to them.

But today they had to ride together to the banquet planning meeting. She was dreading it. Rebecca had to have figured out what had happened when she realized she'd mixed up the folders on the meeting table. No one besides Susan could have picked it up.

Did Rebecca think she'd taken it on purpose? Did she rightfully think Susan had feelings for Ezra? It was going to be uncomfortable.

And to make it all worse, Sadie had broken her ankle on her porch steps the week before. She'd sent all her information to Susan along with a letter instructing her to take over and finish the planning of the dinner.

Susan had no doubts in her ability to complete the Christmas dinner preparations. But the situation between Ezra and Rebecca and her situation with Ezra was a huge impediment to being able to focus properly on the dinner.

Regardless, she would manage it.

She had poured over Sadie's notes and meeting minutes until she was familiar with everything Sadie had put into motion. And she now knew what remained to be taken care of.

The library provided a phone the Amish community could use when needed, so she had a way to make the necessary calls and arrangements. She wouldn't mind being put in charge at all if she didn't have so much tension with everyone except Mary.

Regardless, it was her responsibility to manage it, and she would do it.

She gathered all the information and put it in her bag. She was ready to go whenever Ezra hitched his horse.

To his credit, Ezra made small talk on the drive to the library, and she did her best to sound lighthearted. The weather had warmed enough that the drive wasn't bad at all. She managed to relax a little on the way.

"Are you ready for the meeting?" he asked.

She glanced at him, surprised that he'd switched to a more serious topic. "I believe so. I've gone over everything multiple times. Once Mary and Rebecca give updates, I'll know where we stand. I want to finalize everything today. Then I can place any remaining orders."

"*Gut*. I figured you had it all under control. I know this dinner is an important event for the community."

"We may have to stay later than usual so I can make phone calls," she said.

"That's *nee* problem." He grinned. "I can see you running your own business. You'd be a great boss lady."

She laughed, surprised at his compliment. "I don't know

about that. I guess I could run a little business for myself. But I'd never want to be a boss gal."

"I bet you could do it though."

"Maybe. I guess. I don't know." She laughed, too. And suddenly things seemed to be normal between them again. It was almost like someone had thrown a switch and everything had reset.

The rest of the drive was pleasant, and she was able to relax. There was no need for her to be stressed. Mary was in her corner, and so was Ezra. And as far as Rebecca went, it didn't matter if she was angry or not. Susan hadn't intentionally taken her folder. And if she had not been acting badly, she wouldn't have gotten into hot water with Ezra.

By the time they arrived, Susan was ready to take on whatever came her way. The banquet was a community event that all the youth looked forward to attending. They were always carefully planned. This one would be no different. It was her duty to see to it, and she would.

When they went into the meeting room, Mary and Rebecca were already there pouring over documents.

"Hi," Mary said and smiled.

Rebecca nodded.

And Susan knew everything was going to be fine. The last remaining weight in her chest lifted, and she smiled. "Are we ready to finalize everything and give our youth one of the best dinners ever?"

Rebecca nodded.

"*Jah*, we're ready," Mary said.

"Okay, then. Let's do this," Susan said.

Ezra looked at Susan and smiled. She wasn't sure what she saw in his smile, but it was different this time.

She lifted a questioning eyebrow. But he just smiled again and opened his own folder.

By the time they arrived back home, Susan felt elated. Everything had gone without a hitch. They'd finalized everything. She had indeed felt tension from Rebecca but not hostility, and they'd worked together without any problems.

She'd stayed and made half a dozen phone calls to make sure everything was in place and would be ready for the dinner.

She decided to prepare a special dinner for Ezra and Naomi to celebrate their success. They should invite Nancy over, too.

"Ezra, will you run over and ask Nancy to come over for dinner at seven tonight?"

"I will," he said.

"Tell her I'm fixing a celebration dinner because of the banquet planning so she knows it's going to be something *gut*."

He laughed. "Your food is always *gut*. I think you could turn bare corn cobs into something *gut*."

She laughed. "I wish that was true. But you must have *gut* ingredients to begin with."

He snorted. "I still think you could do it."

She rolled her eyes. "Just go ask Nancy over. Now I must think up something special."

"I will go," he said and bowed low.

"Go on silly," she said.

She watched him pull on his boots and head outside without a coat. She shook her head. Men were interesting creatures. Especially Ezra.

She headed for the kitchen to plan an impromptu feast.

Naomi was in the kitchen baking pies from frozen berries.

"How did your meeting go?" Naomi said.

"So well that I want to fix a celebration dinner for us. I told Ezra to ask Nancy over, too."

Naomi nodded. "Sounds *wunderbaar*. I'll help."

"You don't have to. I can do it all," Susan said.

"I know you can," Naomi said with approval in her voice. "But I want to help."

Susan smiled. "Okay then, let's make a dinner that will be remembered."

"What shall we make?" Naomi asked.

That was so *gut*," Nancy said. "Thanks again for asking me over for dinner."

"You're welcome over here anytime," Naomi said. "And thank you, Ezra, for gathering some holly branches to decorate the table. With my red candle, it's beginning to look like Christmas."

Dinner had turned out perfectly. They had dined on roast chicken with stuffing, potato filling, scalloped potatoes, canned green beans, corn fritters, apple dumplings, and the berry pies. They'd had more food than they could even think about eating.

"We'll fix a leftovers box you can take home if you want," Naomi said. "We have plenty, and you have everything to take care of over there until your husband makes it back home."

"I would love that," Nancy said. "*Denke*."

"Have you any word about when he may be home?" Susan said.

"*Jah*, he said he'll be home for Christmas," Nancy said.

"That's *wunderbaar*," Susan said. "I'm so happy for you. You must bring him over."

"I will," Nancy said. "He'll love meeting all of you."

Susan glanced over and Ezra was staring at her. He smiled, and she couldn't help but smile back.

She was more than happy with how her day had gone. And now, being surrounded by good friends made it even better. Would her parents be surprised at how well things had worked out? She'd been unhappy when they'd told her she would have to stay with Naomi. But now, she knew it was the best thing they could have done for her.

Naomi had become like another grandmother to her. The two of them had forged a bond that would remain for the rest of their lives. Naomi was a wealth of wisdom that can only come from living a long life.

And she'd met Ezra, who was just wonderful. She knew her parents hadn't envisioned anyone coming to stay with them. Maybe they wouldn't have left her there had they known, but she liked him much more than she wanted to admit.

Nancy was a godsend because one day, Susan would have to return home. Now she wouldn't have to worry about Naomi being alone with Nancy right next door.

These people were all important to her, and they always would be.

They might not be blood family, but they were still her family. She'd wondered why her parents were the ones called to go help family when there were other relatives who were closer. But now she understood. Now it all made sense. And everything was just as it was supposed to be.

Chapter Twelve

The day of the Christmas banquet was cold but dry. The roads were clear of snow, and the atmosphere was festive as Christmas had grown nearer. Ezra had attached jingle bells to his horse's harness, and they jingled merrily as the horse trotted toward their destination.

"I hope everything goes well tonight," Susan said.

"It's going to go fine," Ezra said. "That's why we're getting there hours early, to oversee the last-minute preparations. If anything goes wrong, we have time to correct it."

Susan and Ezra arrived at the venue and the buggy area was almost empty. Ezra unharnessed his horse and tied him to the wagon.

"I'll be with you in just a minute," Ezra said and put a blanket over his horse to keep him comfortable out in the open. After he double checked the straps and buckles, he turned to Susan. "Let's go."

They walked to the venue and let themselves in. People were scurrying around and getting everything ready for the dinner.

Mary was already there, and Rebecca arrived soon after. She had a serious look about her, but she concentrated on the job of making sure the dinner went smoothly.

Even Sadie hobbled in on crutches to see how everything was going.

The tables were beautiful with a poinsettia and glass ornaments arranged around the gold foil covered pot as the center piece on sparkling white linen tablecloths.

The scent of delicious food hung in the air like a welcome mist.

The huge room had been decorated in green, gold, and red. Wall tables held clusters of white candles amid fresh cut pine and cedar boughs.

Everything was beautiful.

Sadie was thrilled. It was going to be a wonderful evening.

"Congratulations," Sadie said. "You took charge and did a fantastic job. Everything is lovely."

"*Denke*," Susan said. She was elated at how well things looked.

She said a silent prayer of thanks. The community's youth were going to have a good dinner and evening.

The afternoon passed swiftly with no major issues. And now the first of the community's youth were starting to arrive.

Susan and Ezra moved to the other side of the room. They weren't serving as chaperones so there was no reason to remain where the space was needed for the other youth. They sat at a small round table in the far corner where they could talk and keep an eye on things in case they were needed to take care of something.

"I'm thirsty," Ezra said. "Would you like a soda?"

"That would be great," she said.

"I'll go get us a couple of colas," he said. "I'll be back in a few minutes."

He hurried off to find ice and beverages. But before he found them, he ran into Rebecca.

"Hey," she said. "I wanted to apologize to you. I should have told you everything from the beginning."

"*Jah*, you should have been upfront about it," he said.

"I know. I'm sorry. I truly am. You belong with Susan. I see the way the two of you look at one another."

He cocked his head. Was it so obvious that others saw it? Did his grandmother see it, too? He'd noticed her watching them with an amused expression more than once.

"Anyway," Rebecca said, "I felt like I needed to tell you that, and to offer an apology for wasting your time. David and I are still writing to each other. And he's thinking about relocating to be closer to me."

"Does he have some place to stay?" he said.

"He'll be staying with his *aenti's* and *onkel's familye*. He's making all the arrangements."

"I see," he said.

She offered a small smile. He understood her kindness in explaining things further. And it was time for her to move on—for him, too. "I wish you the best of luck. I hope you find what you're looking for."

"Thank you," she said. "I hope so, too." And with that, she turned and walked away.

He watched her retreating back. It was good that she'd been honest. She had tried to patch things up when she'd come to his grandmother's house. When he wouldn't go along with it, she must have decided it was a sign that she should choose David. But who knew? He hoped she had a nice life.

He hurried on to find something to drink. He eventually found the small kitchen where he was able to get two cups of ice and two cans of cola.

The rental hall didn't provide food to the people who rented it. Food had to be arranged from another party. But in their case, several families did the cooking. The community paid for the food and volunteers prepared it.

He hurried back to the main hall and the table where Susan was waiting for him. Ezra set the cups of ice and cans of soda on the table. He opened the cans and poured the cola over the ice.

"I was starting to wonder if something had happened," Susan said, sounding a bit concerned.

"I'm sorry. Rebecca stopped me to talk."

A look of dread crossed her face.

"The guy she was writing to is coming to live with his *aenti* and *onkel* so he can be near her."

He took a sip of cola and cleared his throat. "Susan..." He suddenly felt awkward, and a knot formed in his stomach, which was ridiculous.

"*Jah?*" She furrowed her brow.

"I really like you," he blurted out like an innocent schoolboy.

She lifted her eyebrows. She hadn't expected him to say that. Then she smiled. "I like you, too. We've had a lot of fun together."

He did his best to settle himself so they could have a serious conversation. He reached and caught her hand in his. "I think you're *wunderbaar*. And beautiful. We get along well, and my feelings for you have been growing."

She looked startled.

Oh, no, he thought. Maybe he shouldn't have said all that. He'd thought she liked him the same way he liked her. Was he wrong?

"I-I was hoping that maybe you would consider going out with me?"

"Let's not rush," she said. She sounded like she was picking her words carefully.

What did that mean?

"I'm not saying I won't," she said. "I'm saying I need to think about it a bit. And I think maybe I should talk to Naomi about it."

His heart sank. She was going to turn him down. He just knew it.

She squeezed his hand. "I do have feelings for you, Ezra. I just want to make sure this is right for both of us."

"I understand," he said. But he didn't understand at all. He liked her, and she liked him. Why shouldn't they court?

Susan would rather Ezra had waited until the dinner was over and they were back at the house. Now she was distracted and unable to concentrate on the event.

She had feelings for him, too. She wouldn't deny that at all. She'd been jealous when Rebecca had come by and talked to him in private. She wouldn't deny that either. But now that he'd admitted his own feelings, it had scared her. She wasn't sure why. Especially because she *did* like him. But courting was serious. And now she was confused.

She knew he was confused by her reaction as well. She hadn't wanted to stall him, but she really needed to talk to Naomi.

She did her best to keep an eye on the dinner party. Lots of guests had arrived, and their conversations filled her ears as a low undercurrent of sound. They would eat soon, and then they would play games and sing carols. It would be a great night for the young people of the community. She was proud that she'd been a part of bringing it about. It was something she would always remember.

Chapter Thirteen

Susan had slept later than usual, not that it was late. She glanced at the clock on the bedside stand. It was almost seven o'clock.

They had stayed until the very end of the dinner and beyond. Everyone had been having so much fun that they had just enjoyed watching from their side table. And then, of course, there was the clean-up.

Sadie had left early. She'd been pleased with the job they'd all done. After congratulating them, she'd been driven home by her brother.

Now, Susan yawned and rubbed her eyes. She had to get up and get moving. They had animals to feed and water. And she needed to talk to Naomi. Because now, after a good night's sleep, she felt even more confused and doubtful.

She got herself moving. Maybe she was just scared. It was a possibility. She dressed and hurried downstairs.

Naomi was already in the kitchen putting on coffee. "Look outside," she said.

Susan had suspected more snow would fall during the night. The air had been laden with it. She had been right. It was deep and clean. "We've had a lot of snow this winter. And it's been really cold."

"We used to have bad winters like this all the time," Naomi said. "Now it's hit or miss. Some winters are colder than others. I remember when I was a little girl, one winter we dug snow tunnels around the yard and crawled through them." Naomi laughed. "It's funny, I can remember that like it was yesterday. We had so much fun crawling through those tunnels."

"*Kinner* have fun with the simplest things," Susan said. "But I have to be honest, I think I would like to do that now."

Naomi nodded. "Me, too. Except these old bones wouldn't appreciate it one bit. I'd be stuck out there in a snow drift." She chuckled. "Wouldn't that be a sight, my feet sticking out of a big drift?"

"I don't know," Susan said. "But I don't think we should test it to find out."

Naomi nodded. "I think I'll stay in here beside the stove and keep warm."

Susan nodded. "Speaking of the stove, I'll get breakfast started."

Naomi sat at the table.

"Can I talk to you about something personal?" Susan said.

"You can talk to me about anything," Naomi said.

"I... Well, I'm confused about Ezra," Susan said. "He confessed to having feelings for me."

"And how do you feel about that?" Naomi asked, her eyes twinkling.

"I don't know," Susan said. "I mean, I do know. I have feelings for him, too. But I don't know what to do."

Naomi gazed at her and nodded. "I remember back when I was about your age. My dear Daniel scared me to death. He wanted to court, but I wasn't sure of what I wanted. I was afraid I was making a mistake. But in the end, I listened to my heart. The heart always knows *nee* matter what the head says. Had I refused, I would have made the biggest mistake of my life. I married him eventually, and we had so many years of love, and everything that goes with it."

Susan nodded.

"You know," Naomi said, "marriage isn't just loving someone. That's the easy part. There are disagreements, moments of anger, even regret sometimes. But that's just the head talking. The heart doesn't pay attention to those things, and they always pass quickly. The heart always knows the truth of the situation. *Nee* matter what the brain comes up with, the heart tells the truth."

Naomi nodded as if to herself. "So, my advice is...and I would tell Ezra the exact same thing...listen to your heart. Because it already knows the truth, *nee* matter which way that truth lies. The heart knows what it is. Even if the brain tries to lie, it can't fool the heart."

"I actually think I understand exactly what you're telling me," Susan said.

"I knew you would. Don't rush. Listen to what your heart whispers to you late at night or early in the morning or when you're working on something and least expect to hear the heart speak. Those unexpected times...that's when the heart speaks up and tells you the truth of a situation."

"I wish you were my *grossmammi*," Susan said. "I feel like you are."

"Susan, you can consider me another *grossmammi* if you like. In fact, I'd be honored if you did." Then she laughed. "But you should be glad I'm not, since Ezra is my *grosskinner*."

Susan grinned. "You have a point."

"That said," Naomi said, "*nee* one could ask for a better granddaughter than you. You've been such a blessing to me. I'll be honest, there's nothing I'd like more than for you and

Ezra to court and marry. But you must listen to your heart. It will tell you what's best for you."

"All right, that's what I'm going to do," Susan said. "And now I'm going to fix us all some breakfast."

Over the next few days, Ezra went out of his way to be helpful and show Susan affection. Susan found it endearing. He was like a puppy, constantly under her feet and clamoring for her attention.

In another sense, it was the strangest thing she'd ever experienced.

He bought a box of fancy chocolates, which she shared with all of them. At every turn, he offered to help her with whatever she was doing. There was no doubt that he wanted to court, and he was persistent about it.

Naomi just watched and shook her head with a little smile.

Susan had just finished dusting when Ezra got home from visiting a friend. To her surprise, he didn't immediately start offering to do things for her.

Had his friend talked some sense into him? Maybe. It would be nice if things went back to the way they had been before he told her how he felt. He didn't need to go to extremes. He just needed to be himself. That was what she wanted.

To her relief, later in the day, he caught up with her in the kitchen.

"Susan," he said, "I want to apologize. I know I've been acting like a fool these last few days. I talked with my friend, and he set me straight. I know I can't force you to love me. I wasn't trying to do that. I was just hoping you cared for me, too. So, I'll just let things be and either things will happen, or they won't."

"I talked to your *Grossmammi*," Susan said. "She advised me, and I'm taking her advice. I think we just need to let things go as they will. Time will tell what is right for us."

He nodded. If they were meant to be, it would happen. Her heart would tell her what was true.

She had feelings for him, she was aware of that. But were they enough for a serious relationship? Were they love? That was what she had to be sure of. Was she afraid of the overwhelming emotions tugging at her and the changes in her life a serious relationship would bring? She hadn't expected such confusion and turmoil.

She decided to focus on Christmas and think about what she wanted in a relationship later. She needed to finish up her gifts for Naomi and Ezra. The only time she was able to work on them was when she was in her room at night. She needed to turn in early over the next few nights to get them finished in time for Christmas.

It would give her time to consider things and listen to her heart, too. Naomi was right. Her head was a mess with thoughts running amok and making her apprehensive and indecisive. Her heart would guide her and show her the answers she needed.

She was far from being a fool. Not all pairings were good, and she didn't want to be locked into something like that. But love wasn't something to run from. either. It was something to run to. And just maybe, Ezra was the one to run to.

Chapter Fourteen

"Let's get some pine boughs and decorate a bit more for Christmas. *Grossmammi* has lots of white candles we could use," Ezra said.

"Sure," Susan said. "Why not? I have some red, satin ribbon we can use, too." The house would look more festive and smell nice for Christmas if they decorated with fresh-cut pine and cedar boughs and accented them with candles and ribbon.

They pulled on their outdoor clothing and went out into the biting wind. They stopped at the shed, and Ezra grabbed the handsaw. "We should take the sled. I don't fancy carrying a bunch of branches back."

"*Gut* idea," she said. "Grab it, and I'll pull it."

The sled leaned against the back wall. He grabbed it and hauled it out for her. "It's light. You shouldn't have any problem with it. Or I'd be happy to pull it."

She took the rope and tested it. The sled skated easily over the snow. "All *gut*. Let's go." They headed toward the large stand of trees a short distance from the back of Naomi's house. They could find more than enough greenery to decorate with.

They crossed a large open field and suddenly Ezra dropped the saw, scooped up a handful of snow and threw it at her. It caught her on the shoulder. He laughed and grinned—openly inviting her to return fire.

"You're going to get it now," she yelled and burst into laughter. She dropped the sled rope and whisked up a double handful of snow, packing it into a ball. She slung it at him, catching him on the arm.

"It's on now," he yelled back.

And then both were scooping up and throwing snowballs while laughing uproariously at each other. They kept it up until both were covered in snow and they were panting for breath.

Finally, laughing so hard he barely got the words out, Ezra cried, "Truce!"

Giggling, she relented and tossed down the packed snow she held in her hand. "Okay, but I won."

"I guess you did at that," he said through another burst of laughter.

She brushed herself off. "I can't remember the last time I had so much fun."

"Me, neither," Ezra said and retrieved the handsaw. "But I guess we better get on with getting some greenery. Otherwise, you're going to clobber me even worse."

"*Jah*, and don't you forget it," she said and snickered again.

They walked companionably to the trees and cut some low branches to avoid damaging the beauty of the evergreens. Once they had enough to decorate, they loaded the last of them on the sled, and he took the rope.

"I can pull it," she said.

"I know you can, but why? I'll do it."

She shrugged. "Okay then. Let's go make the *haus* pretty."

By the time they returned to the house, Naomi had the candles out and the best places to decorate ready. She had taken off the items that normally sat where the greenery would go and stored them until after the holidays.

"This will be so pretty," she said. "I haven't had the *haus* so decorated since... Well, it's been a while."

Susan knew she had meant there'd been hardly any decorating since her husband died. Her stomach knotted. Why didn't someone come decorate for her? Well, her parents' home wasn't far away. She would make certain Naomi's home was decorated from now on. She glanced at Ezra, and she was pretty sure he was thinking something similar.

They set to work and soon the house smelled fragrant, and the candle flames danced merrily.

Naomi clasped her hands and said, "It's beautiful."

Indeed, it was. Susan looked at Ezra and smiled at him. He smiled back. He was so handsome, especially when he smiled. She wasn't sure what had motivated Rebecca to fancy another man when Ezra was so perfect. He was…

She caught herself.

Listen to your heart.

She was listening.

Susan forked over a strip of bacon and glanced out the kitchen window. "Christmas Eve already," Susan said. "Are you sure you don't want to go to the school's Christmas program?"

"I'm sure, dear," Naomi said. "It's too cold for these old bones to go out if I don't have to."

"I understand that," Susan said and turned more bacon strips over.

Ezra came in and poured a huge cup of coffee. He sat at the table and stirred sugar and cream into the coffee.

"The *haus* smells *gut*. Between the bacon, *kaffe*, and evergreen, it smells like Christmas in a kitchen."

Susan laughed. "That's silly."

"Still smells great in here," he said.

"You kids should take a blanket tonight," Naomi said. "It's going to be really cold. Might snow more, too. You can feel it in the air already."

"Snow on Christmas is always welcome," Ezra said. "I know we already have a lot, but it's all tracked up from walking through it. I'd love to get up in the morning to a pure white layer."

"You may get your wish," Naomi said with a little smile.

The three of them spent most of the day in the kitchen. Susan and Naomi baked cookies and pumpkin pies for their Christmas dinner. And Ezra just stayed and chatted with them.

"The smell of those sugar cookies is driving me half mad," he said and grinned.

"They're still pretty hot, but you're welcome to take as many as you want," Susan said. "We have enough dough for another batch."

"Thanks," he said and grabbed three cookies off the cookie sheet.

Naomi rolled her eyes. "You're going to turn into a cookie."

"Probably," he said.

"You need to keep an eye on him," Naomi said to Susan. "Before he eats us out of *haus* and home." She smiled to show she was kidding.

"Who owns the property next door?" Ezra said and nodded his head to the left.

"That's the Weiss' place. Why?" Naomi said.

"I saw a *for sale* sign in their yard," he said.

Naomi nodded. "They'll have a tough time selling it. The house needs repairs, and the land isn't *gut* for farming."

"How did they make a living?" Ezra said.

"Mr. Weiss has a nice workshop, and he makes furniture. I guess he wants to retire and move where his son lives in the next district over. Can't blame him. It's the only *familye* he has left."

"The house doesn't look bad," Ezra said.

"It isn't bad. It just needs some repairs. Someone with your skills could probably have everything fixed in a few months or so. But the Weisses up there in years, and they've just let it go a bit."

"Well, it might sell quicker than you would think," he said.

"Be nice if a young couple moved in. It would be *gut* to hear *kinner* playing and having fun again before I leave to meet the *gut* Lord."

"Maybe someone like that will buy it. It would be nice if you had some more neighbors to help you out when you need it."

"Well, Nancy is nice, and she's right next door," Naomi said. "I sure hope her husband makes it home tomorrow. She's been alone over there too long."

"I hope so, too," Susan said. "It would be awful if he didn't make it back tomorrow. Nancy had been so excited that he would be home for Christmas. Besides, she needs him there."

"Whoever buys it," Ezra said. "I hope they'll be *gut* neighbors."

"I'm sure they will," Naomi said.

Susan and Ezra arrived for the school Christmas program, and the buggy area was nearly full already. They wouldn't be there too long, so he didn't unharness the horse, but Ezra did put the blanket on him.

The clouds had cleared, and the stars twinkled brightly overhead in the cold night sky.

He helped Susan out of the buggy, and they walked toward the huge barn where the program was going to take place. They crowded into the barn, and it was standing room only. So, they found a place near the back. The spectators were crowded around the area where the performance would take place.

They didn't have to wait long before the lamps were dimmed, and the audience quieted. Then the players came out onto their stage, and the story of the birth of Jesus began.

Susan enjoyed every moment of the play. The students were eager and gave a wonderful performance. She glanced up at Ezra, and he was smiling, too. At the end of the program, everyone gave the players a standing ovation.

"Let's go outside where we can talk for a minute," Ezra said.

"Sure, it's packed in here," she said.

They left the barn and went a little way from the throng of people. Then they walked back to the buggy, and Ezra took the blanket off the horse and folded it. He put it behind the seat then he turned to Susan.

"Let's talk for a minute before we go," he said.

"Sure," Susan said.

"Susan, I'm just going to say it. I love you."

She looked into his eyes, and in the starlight, she saw the truth in them. And she knew that her heart was giving her its truth as well. She knew what her heart wanted.

"I love you, too," she said.

"When do you want to exchange gifts?" Naomi asked.

"How about now," Ezra said.

Naomi laughed. "Whatever you two want to do is okay with me."

"Let's do it now, before we eat dinner," Ezra said.

"Okay," Naomi said. "I'll go get my gifts."

"Me, too," Susan said.

"I hid mine in the parlor," Ezra said.

Susan went to get their gifts from her room. She'd wrapped them in gold paper and put red bows on them. They were pretty packages. Hopefully, they would like what she'd made for them. She hurried back to the kitchen with the packages.

Naomi had two packages.

A moment later Ezra came to the kitchen with two wrapped boxes. "Let me go first."

He handed a box to Naomi. "I hope you like it."

"I'd like anything I received as a gift," Naomi said and smiled at Ezra. She carefully opened the pretty green box. "*Ach* my goodness," she said and grinned.

"What is it?" Susan said.

"New embroidery hoops and so much thread. There are some intricate patterns, too. I love it. *Denke*, Ezra."

Ezra handed the other package to Susan.

"*Ach*, it's heavy," she said.

"Open it."

She tore off the silver paper and pulled out a huge volume of inspirational poetry.

"*Ach*, my goodness. This is beautiful." She looked through a few pages. "*Denke* this is *wunderbaar*. I can't wait to read these."

"I'll go next," Naomi said. "Susan, this is for you." She passed over a box wrapped in red foil.

Susan carefully unwrapped it. It was a lovely journal with a purple and teal silk cover and gold edges on the pages. "*Denke*, Naomi, it's so pretty."

"I'm glad you like it," Naomi said.

"Ezra, this is for you." She gave him a package wrapped in blue foil.

He unwrapped the package and took out a crisp white shirt. "*Denke*. This is really nice."

"You're welcome," Naomi said.

"*Ach*, look," Susan said.

"What is it?" Naomi said.

"It must be Nancy's husband," Susan said as she tried to get a better look. "It is her husband—she just ran out to greet him."

"Thank the Lord," Naomi said. "I'm so happy for her."

"Me, too," Susan said. She'd been afraid he wasn't going to come home. But there he was. Nancy had prepared Christmas dinner in case he made it. And he had.

Susan was even happier now that she knew Nancy's husband had returned.

"Okay," Susan said. "My turn." She passed a larger package to Naomi. "I thought you might like this."

"I'll love anything you gave me," Naomi said and opened the box.

Inside was the lovely lap throw Susan had worked on for many evenings.

"*Ach*, Susan. This is so beautiful. And I can use it. *Denke*."

"Ezra, this is for you." She handed the last package to him.

Ezra ripped the package open and lifted out the scarf and hat she had made with autumn's signature colors. "Wow, I love this. *Denke*." He wrapped the scarf around his neck and grinned.

"This is a Christmas I'll never forget," Naomi said.

"I don't think any of us will ever forget this Christmas," Susan said. She would never have thought she could have such a wonderful Christmas without her parents being there. But it was one of the best she'd ever had. The love she felt for the two people who'd shared the day with her had made it special in every way. The love and joy she'd found with them had made it a day she would cherish for the rest of her life.

Epilogue

Christmas, One Year Later

Susan rubbed her expanding belly while her mother and Naomi fussed over the last-minute Christmas dinner preparations. She was so thankful for the blessings the good Lord had given her in the last year.

She glanced out the kitchen window at the fresh blanket of snow that had fallen the night before. From there, the old Weiss property, she could see Naomi's house and beyond that, Nancy's. She had been thrilled when Ezra had purchased the property and set about fixing it up.

She was so happy to be next door to Naomi. Now she could make sure Naomi always had help when she needed it. And it was nice to have a good friend to go spend time with. Naomi had been the first person to learn about the baby they were expecting in the spring.

Hopefully, she and Ezra would have many children over the years. Being his wife was wonderful, and now she couldn't wait to be a mother.

She glanced about the kitchen. She had decorated it in blue, yellow, and white, and she loved it. Ezra had fixed everything that was wrong and added to it. He was talented with carpentry. Her father had been able to help quite a bit as well.

She loved their house. It was big enough to raise a brood of children.

Her father and Ezra were in the parlor while the womenfolk finished dinner. She heard her husband and father laughing uproariously. What were they doing in there that was so funny? Maybe she didn't want to find out. She bit her lip to stop from flashing a big grin.

"Come everyone," her mother called. "Let's eat.

After a delicious Christmas dinner, Ezra and her father looked at each other, and then Ezra said, "We have a surprise."

"What kind of surprise?" her mother said with a suspicious look toward Susan's father.

"It's a *gut* surprise," Ezra said. "We want all of you to get your boots and warm clothes on. We're going to have some fun."

"What are you talking about?" Susan said.

"Just put on warm clothes. You won't regret it. I promise," Ezra said. "We'll be ready out front in just a little bit." Ezra and Susan's father pulled on their boots and coats and went outside.

"Well," Susan said. "I guess we should get our coats and see what they've got in mind."

"I can't imagine what they're up to," her mother said.

"I'd say we're going to find out in a few minutes," Susan said. She pulled on her boots and grabbed her coat.

They stepped outside into the cold and waited on the porch.

"Hey, I hear jingle bells," Naomi said with a smile.

"So do I," Susan said.

"Look!" Susan's mother pointed toward the barn.

Two huge black horses pulled a large sleigh over the snow, coming toward the house. Their breath puffed out as white vapor in the cold air.

"Where did that come from?" Susan said. They didn't have two monster-sized horses. Or at least they hadn't. She wasn't exactly sure what was going on.

Ezra brought the sleigh to the house. "Well, what do you think of them?"

"I'm not sure what I'm supposed to think," Susan said.

"I bought some horses and this sleigh," Ezra said.

"Did you?" she asked, startled. "They're beautiful."

"These horses sell for a lot of money. I got them for a *gut* price, along with the sleigh."

"So, you bought them to resell?" Susan said.

"*Nee*. I have a third horse in the barn. A stallion. I'm going to raise horses as a side business. They sleigh is just for fun. For us."

Susan shook her head, but she smiled at him. If he wanted a side business, it was fine with her. Besides, she loved horses. She eyed up the big animals. "What kind of horses are they?"

"They're Percherons. Well, come on everyone. Get in, and let's go for a ride. There are blankets if anyone wants to wrap up."

"Let's go," Susan said.

Naomi was the first to get in. "I haven't been in a sleigh in so many years."

Susan and her mother climbed in and once everyone was ready, Ezra signaled the big horses to go forward at a ground-eating trot that kicked up snow with each step. The bells on their harness rang merrily. The sleigh glided over the snow.

Ezra drove the team around the back of the property.

The snow glistened like diamonds under the cold sun.

"Look," Naomi said and pointed to a small flock of Cardinals sitting on a bush. Their scarlet feathers puffed out against the cold.

"They're so pretty," Susan said.

"Nature is *God's* gift to us," Naomi said with a little smile.

"It certainly is," Susan's mother said.

Ezra drove around the parameter of their property then headed back to the house.

Susan was glad they didn't stay out too long because even with the blankets, it was still very cold.

Ezra drove them back to the house, and when everyone was out of the sleigh, he headed back to the barn.

"That was fun," Naomi said. "I didn't think I would ever go on another sleigh ride."

"It was fun. But I'm ready to sit around the stove and have some hot chocolate."

Her mother waited until Naomi and Susan were up the porch steps before following them up. "I could go for a nice cup of hot chocolate, too." She rubbed her arms through her coat. "It's really cold today."

They went inside and removed their coats and boots before heading to the kitchen.

Susan put a pot of milk on the burner and got out the tin of cocoa. She stirred it in slowly, keeping the milk moving to avoid scorching it.

She marveled at having such a wonderful Christmas. A new home, a baby on the way, Naomi, her parents, all together. And of course, her wonderful husband. She'd always been happy, and she thought she knew what true happiness was. But this was even better.

Happiness was the people who shared her life. Her community. The good Lord above. Those were the only things she needed to be happy and content. It wouldn't have mattered what house they lived in as long as she had family, friends, and faith to sustain her.

And because now she understood what made a full life—a good life, she understood she had been blessed beyond measure. She looked around the table and smiled as she stirred the hot chocolate.

Life was good. And it would only get better. "I love you all," she said. "My life wouldn't be complete without each of you. I hope we have many more Christmases just like this."

"We will," Ezra said from the doorway. He gave her an easy grin.

"I know you're right," Susan said.

She poured the chocolate into cups for each of them then lifted her own cup. "Merry Christmas. And many more."

The others lifted their mugs and a chorus of "Merry Christmas" rang out in the little kitchen.

Susan smiled at Ezra and sipped the chocolate. Indeed, it was a wonderful Christmas—one she would never forget.

The End

Continue Reading...

Thank you for reading **Christmas Storm!** Are you wondering **what to read next?** Why not read *Sarah's Mistake?* **Here's a peek for you:**

As the clouds overhead suddenly parted to reveal the sun, Sarah Lantz hoped the break in the harsh winter weather would prove to be a good omen. She walked down the main street of Rock Point, Ohio, avoiding the icy patches on the sidewalk and dodging around piles of snow that had been shoveled to the edges of the pavement in front of the row of shops following the most recent storm. The sun now shining brightly overhead caused the mounds of white to sparkle like hundreds of diamonds.

Her breath fogged in front of her in the chilly air, and she tucked her gloved hands into the pockets of her coat. She scarcely noticed the freezing temperature as her mind was occupied with other thoughts.

She prayed things would go better for her here in this unfamiliar community than they had gone for her back home in Russellton, Illinois. She hoped news of her past mistakes would not follow her and ruin her fresh start in this new town.

Hopefully, things couldn't be any worse for her here than the situation she had left behind. Her greatest fear was she wouldn't be able to truly escape what had happened—at least not for long—and that word of the disastrous series of events would somehow become known.

She feared she would be judged unfairly by the people here, just as she had been back home. And no matter how she tried to explain her side of things, everyone would believe that most of the blame should be placed squarely on her.

How could she expect to receive support from strangers when people she had known for years and years had turned their backs on her?

She didn't deny her part in the debacle, but she didn't feel she deserved to shoulder so much of the blame. She had only been trying to help a friend and had believed Naomi truly needed her aid.

Sarah and Naomi Hilty had been best friends since their first day of lessons at the Amish schoolhouse in Russellton when they were six. And even after they left school at age thirteen nearly a decade before, they had remained friends throughout the intervening years.

VISIT HERE To Read More!

https://www.ticahousepublishing.com/amish-miller.html

Thank you for Reading

If you **love Amish Romance**, **Visit Here:**

https://amish.subscribemenow.com/

to find out about all **New Hannah Miller Amish Romance Releases! We will let you know as soon as they become available!**

If you enjoyed ***Christmas Storm,*** would you kindly take a couple minutes to leave a positive review on Amazon? It only takes a moment, and positive reviews truly make a difference. I would be so grateful! Thank you!

Turn the page to discover more Hannah Miller Amish Romances just for you!

More Amish Romance from Hannah Miller

Visit HERE for Hannah Miller's Amish Romance

https://ticahousepublishing.com/amish-miller.html

About the Author

Hannah Miller has been writing Amish Romance for the past seven years. Long intrigued by the Amish way of life, Hannah has traveled the United States, visiting different Amish communities. She treasures her Amish friends and enjoys visiting with them. Hannah makes her home in Indiana, along with her husband, Robert. Together, they have three children and seven grandchildren. Hannah loves to ride bikes in the sunshine. And if it's warm enough for a picnic, you'll find her under the nearest tree!

Made in United States
Troutdale, OR
11/20/2024